The Happy Hollisters and the Ghost Horse Mystery

BY JERRY WEST

Illustrated by Helen S. Hamilton

DOUBLEDAY & COMPANY, INC.
GARDEN CITY, NEW YORK

The author thanks The National Audubon Society for its courteous assistance in the preparation of this story.

Contents

CHAPTER 1

The Pink Sea Gull

"Look! A big pink bird!" Pam Hollister cried out. "It's lying by the side of the road. Please stop!"

The driver frowned. "Are you sure?"

"Oh yes! We must go back and help it," Pam begged. "Please, Indy."

The station wagon turned around and headed in the opposite direction on the New England highway. Indy's cargo included the five Hollister children, his sister Emmy, and his cocker spaniel, Blackie.

"There it is!" Pam exclaimed. The car stopped and the girl got out. She crossed the highway and lifted a big pink bird into her arms. As she hastened back the children gasped. Even Indy and Emmy looked amazed.

"It's a sea gull. A pink sea gull!" Emmy said. "I just can't believe it!"

"Do you think somebody painted it for fun?" asked Ricky, to whom the idea might naturally occur.

"Of course not," Holly replied. "Nobody paints birds."

The six-year-old pigtailed girl kneeled in the middle of the back seat between twelve-year-old Pete and Pam, who was ten. Both were blond, but the boy's hair was crew cut and his sister's was fluffy. Behind them amid the suitcases and blankets sprawled red-haired Ricky, seven, and next to him sat four-year-old Sue with her arm around Blackie. The dog looked over Pam's shoulder at the bird, and gave a low *woof!*

The driver was Indy Roades, a real Indian from New Mexico. His sister Emmy, an attractive young woman, was seated beside him. Indy had moved East some years before, and now worked in the store owned by Mr. Hollister in Shoreham. Emmy had come to visit her brother, and the two had agreed to take the youngsters on a trip to solve a mystery. They had already done this, and, relaxed and happy, were on their way back to Shoreham. Now a new adventure had popped up in the form of a pink sea gull.

The bird lay contentedly in Pam's lap and blinked its eyes now and then.

Emmy, meanwhile, studied the map in her lap and said, "There's a big town about five miles up the road. We can stop there and make an inquiry about the sea gull."

"Okay," Pam said as she stroked the bird's head.

A stop light halted the vacationers as they entered the town, and Indy asked a policeman standing nearby if there was anybody who knew about pink sea gulls.

"You're fooling," the officer said with a smile as he glanced in at the five youngsters.

"No, we're not," Pam said. "Look here."

2

The policeman's eyes widened. Then he said, "The Audubon Society has a place on the other side of town. It's right beside the highway. You can't miss it. Maybe they can help you."

"Thank you," Indy said, and drove on as the light turned green.

"What's an odd bon?" asked Sue.

"You mean Audubon Society," Pam told her. "It's an organization of people who study and protect birds."

"The Society is named for John James Audubon," Pete added. "He was an early American naturalist who explored the wilderness to observe birds, and made beautiful paintings of them."

"I'll bet he never saw a pink sea gull," remarked Holly.

After riding through traffic for about fifteen minutes the travelers came to an arrow sign pointing into a driveway. Off the highway stood a low red brick building. Alongside it was a garage and behind it several wire pens.

"This must be the place," Pete said. The car stopped in the drive and they all got out except Blackie. Ricky held the door open for Emmy and Indy to enter, and the children followed into an office.

Seated behind a desk was a young woman. She glanced at Pam and the bird and said, "Oh, so you found one! Wait a minute, please, and I'll call Mr. Landon." She picked up the telephone and several seconds later a tall man came through a door at the rear of the room. He had a high forehead, a boyish face, and a rugged outdoors look. Behind him was a young man of eighteen with sandy hair and a big smile.

"I'm Jim Landon," the tall man said, extending his hand to Indy. "This is Gary Dale," he added, indicating the boy. After the visitors had introduced themselves, Jim Landon took the sea gull from Pam and looked at it carefully. "Driven in by the storm, I guess," he said, "and exhausted— that's all." With a smile he let Pam hold the bird again.

"But—but it's pink!" Pam said.

"Oh, sure," Mr. Landon said casually. "This is one of the birds we colored on the coast."

"You mean you paint sea gulls?" Pete asked in disbelief.

"Yikes! Tell us about it!" Ricky said.

"I'll be glad to. Come in and sit down," the man replied cordially. He ushered them through the rear door into a large exhibit room. Around the walls were cases filled with stuffed birds and on several open perches sat other birds, looking very natural. Sue wandered off to inspect them as the rest of the travelers listened intently to the bird-man.

Mr. Landon explained that several years before an airplane had crashed because sea gulls had been sucked into the jet engine. As a result the Audubon Society was making a study of the habits of these birds. "We hire college students in the

4

summer to trap and color them," the man said. "Red, green, blue, and yellow paint is used, but the red fades to pink because of the bright sun and the salt water. The dye is harmless, of course."

Gary Dale spoke up enthusiastically. "I'm one of those who catch and color the birds!" He explained that he was on his way to an island called Wicket-ee-nock. "I'm going to meet a boy and girl there who are the rest of my gull-painting team," he explained. "We live in tents."

"But how do you catch sea gulls?" asked Pete.

"We use net traps and fish lines—without hooks, of course."

"Yikes! I'd like to catch some," Ricky said.

"And paint them too," Holly added brightly. "Can we go with you, Gary?"

A serious look came over the young man's face and he shook his head. "I don't think that would be wise," he said.

"Why not?" blurted Ricky.

The Audubon men exchanged looks. "There's no harm in telling, I guess," said Gary. "There's a mystery on the island."

"Mystery!" Pete exclaimed. "What is it?"

Gary replied that the last sea-gull-coloring team had been scared off by a ghost horse.

"A ghost horse!" Pam said. "You mean it?"

Gary nodded. "They say it's a frightening thing—a small white animal. I've never seen it myself."

5

"Maybe we could solve the mystery for you," said Holly.

Mr. Landon smiled. "Are you detectives?" he asked, expecting the answer to be No.

The Hollisters nodded Yes, and Indy quickly told about the most recent case they had solved.

"But it's time we were getting home," Emmy put in. "I'm afraid we couldn't stay on the island more than a day. That's not long enough to solve a mystery," she added with a smile, "even for my favorite detectives."

"But we might find a clue for Gary," Pam said "Please let us try."

"We certainly could use some help on the mystery," said Mr. Landon, and Gary agreed.

The Hollisters turned pleading eyes on Indy "All right," he said, "but just for one night and one day."

Holly gave Indy a bear hug, and the other children chorused excited "Thank-yous!"

"It's not far from here," Gary told them. "We can make Cliffport by sundown. That's where we get the ferry to the island."

While the other children chattered happily about the trip, Sue wandered off to the far side of the room. There she went up to a low perch on which sat a small owl. Curious, she moved closer, almost touching it. Then she put out a chubby finger and poked at the bird. The owl toppled, but only for a second. As Sue cried out, it spread its wings and flew around the room.

6

"Oh! It's not stuffed!" the little girl exclaimed as the bird came to rest on her left shoulder. The other Hollisters were startled, but not Mr. Landon or Gary.

"That's a tame screech owl," the birdman said. "We call her Fluffy." As he set the bird back on the perch, he explained that he had found it injured on Wicket-ee-nock Island. "I think she fell out of the nest," he said. "I nursed her and fed her by hand. That's why she's not afraid of you," he added to Sue.

The little dark-haired girl reached out and petted the owl with one finger.

Indy watched her with a smile, then turned to Gary. "We'd better be leaving. Is your baggage ready?"

Eagerly the boy led them to the next room, where his things lay in a pile on the floor. Besides suitcases and blankets, his gear included a rope, which he explained was for climbing steep rocky places, and a bundle of long cardboard tubes tied together.

"What are these?" Ricky asked. "Fireworks?"

"They're flares," replied Gary. "If a guller gets into a dangerous spot he uses those to signal for help. They work like Roman candles."

"Yikes!" exclaimed Ricky. "I wish I could fire one!"

"What's this, Gary?" asked Holly, pointing to a large metal frame covered with net. "It looks like a big clam."

"Oh! It's not stuffed!"

"That's a sea-gull trap." Gary opened the halves of the "clam" all the way, so that they met again back to back. He secured them by fastening an attached metal rod across them.

"You put this trap next to the nest," he explained. "When the bird touches it, the rod is released and half the net springs up and comes down over the gull. Then we take him out."

"How do you color him?" asked Holly.

"You'd better wait and see us do it," the boy said with a wink.

While Gary Dale was putting his things into the well-loaded station wagon, he told them that he had painted gulls on Wicket-ee-nock the year before.

"The island's owned by Cadwallader Clegg," he said.

"Who?" asked Ricky.

"Cadwallader Clegg. He's a funny old fellow—the one-man police force in Cliffport."

When all of Gary's things were stowed away, Pam carefully handed the sea gull over to Mr. Landon.

"As soon as he gets well, I'll turn him loose," the man said.

"I wish we could take Fluffy along," Sue piped up.

"I wish you could, too," replied Mr. Landon with a smile. "The owl is strong enough now to forage for herself. She really ought to be set free where I found her."

9

"Oh," said Holly, "we'd be glad to do it, wouldn't we, Indy?"

With a grin, Indy agreed and Sue clapped her hands. Mr. Landon hurried inside and soon came out with the owl in a metal cage. As he put it in the rear of the car, he told Gary to bring the empty cage back.

The travelers said good-by and the station wagon started toward Cliffport.

A short time later Indy stopped at a roadside restaurant and they all had supper. It was nearly sundown when they reached a road which led along the top of a steep cliff.

"There's Wicket-ee-nock," declared Gary. Across the gleaming water they could see the long dark shape of the island. Ahead the road dipped down to the town of Cliffport. "And that's Cadwallader Clegg's place," the boy added, pointing to a house near the rim of the cliff.

Indy drove into the driveway and the children got out. Ricky ran toward the cliff edge with Holly and Blackie at his heels.

"Be careful!" Emmy called out.

"We will! Don't worry," Ricky replied.

"We're going to catch a green sea gull," Holly added as the others went up onto the porch of the house.

Pete knocked on the door. It was answered by an old man with flowing white hair. He was tall and spare and his light blue eyes looked piercingly at the boy.

"No visitors on Wicket-ee-nock," he said. "My tenants want privacy."

"But wait," said Pete as Indy stepped to his side.

"We want to help Gary Dale catch sea gulls and paint them," the Indian spoke up.

"Oh," the man said. "More Audubon Society people, eh?"

"Yes," Gary said, pulling a paper from his pocket to identify himself. "I have to meet Bill and Jane Lesser. They're the other part of my gull-painting team."

Cadwallader Clegg fingered the shiny badge on his suspenders as he thought for a moment. Then he motioned the visitors inside his house.

"We just want to stay overnight," Indy explained as they entered. "We'll—" He was interrupted by shouting and barking outside.

"Oh dear, what's happened?" said Emmy. As she turned to the door, Ricky dashed in followed by Holly and Blackie.

"We saw it! We saw it!" the redhead cried.

"Saw what?" Pete demanded.

"The ghost horse!"

CHAPTER 2

A Spyglass View

"STEADY now," said Cadwallader Clegg, placing one big bony hand on Ricky's shoulder and the other on Holly's. "There's no such a thing as a ghost horse!"

"But we saw it," insisted Ricky, panting.

"Now, Ricky," Emmy said, "are you sure you didn't imagine it?"

"Holly saw it, too," he declared, and his sister nodded her head so hard her braids bounced.

"What did it look like?" asked Pete.

"It was white," said Holly, "and it was standing up on some rocks."

"In that case," said Cadwallader, "we'd better look for this mysterious horse."

Cadwallader Clegg took a long telescope and tripod from the corner of the room and marched outdoors, the others trailing behind him. He set up the instrument on the edge of the cliff and squinted through the eyepiece at Wicket-ee-nock Island.

"I don't see any horse," he said, and motioned to Emmy. "Here, take a look for yourself."

Emmy scanned the island, then her brother looked. Next Pam put her eye to the long telescope. Her gaze crept back and forth over the island. It was long and sandy with rocky points at both ends. In the middle, facing the mainland, was a wide beach. To the left of it stood a white frame house, and behind that was a huge barn perched high on a rock cliff looking out to the ocean. To the right of the beach, Pam noticed an old dilapidated inn. She could even make out the broken shingle with a faded red lobster painted on it.

As Pam watched, a small ferryboat, perhaps big enough to hold three cars, pulled away from a dock on Wicket-ee-nock and started for the mainland, trailing a thin white wake.

"It's my turn to look," clamored Ricky.

"Me, too," said Holly.

"You'll all have a turn," Pete said. Politely, he waited until last. After holding up little Sue for a look, he placed her on the ground and peered through the telescope. He scanned the island carefully, but, like the others, saw no sign of the white horse.

As they walked back to the station wagon, Emmy asked Cadwallader Clegg where they could get bedding for their stay on the island.

"I have cots for rent," he said, "and I'll give you clean pillows, linen, and blankets with them. You can sleep in the deserted inn," he added with a grin, "if you don't mind a few cobwebs."

When the bedding had been stowed in the station wagon and the cots lashed to the roof, the travelers thanked Cadwallader Clegg for his hos-

13

pitality. Even little Sue gave the man's gnarled hand a good hard shake.

"I wish you luck," Cadwallader said as they got into the station wagon. "Don't forget your promise about the tenants on my island. And beware of the ghost horse," he called. They heard him chuckle as Indy drove away.

The road wound like a serpent down the cliff-side until it reached Cliffport, nestled against the water below. The town was tiny, with a few homes and stores and a little church with a white steeple. To the left of the dock, Pete noticed a small motel and to the right was a shack with the sign "Boats for Hire." And on the pier itself was a man with a small handcart. On its side were big red letters which said, "Try the Snowman's famous snow-sticks."

As Indy parked the station wagon in front of the motel the man trundled his pushcart beside it.

"I'm the Snowman!" the stout jovial fellow announced. His quick eyes took in the five youngsters. "Shall that be five snow-sticks?" he asked, beaming.

"Make it eight," said Indy. "We'll all have a treat."

The Snowman pulled back the lid and took out the white ice-cream sticks. Sue, the first to receive hers, slid off the paper cover and her little red tongue licked the frosty treat. This left a chocolate spot.

The Snowman, noticing her expression, said,

14

"I'm the Snowman!"

"Aha, I knew you'd like my snow-sticks!" He told her they were iced with candy on the outside, had chocolate under that, and then vanilla ice cream.

"They're yummy!" Holly said, and her teeth crunched into the snow-stick.

Just then the dock gave a little shudder as the ferryboat pulled into a slip at the far end of it.

Careful not to drop their ice cream, the children got out of the station wagon and ran to see the boat with Gary following them. Pete was disappointed that it carried no cars. The only persons aboard were the ferryman and two young people.

As the man jumped off and secured a stout Manila line, Gary called out to the two passengers. "Hi, Bill! Hi, Jane! I was just coming over to join you on the island."

"Not us, I'm afraid," said Bill as he bent down to pick up his luggage from the deck. His sister Jane, a pretty girl with short dark hair, did the same. They stepped onto the pier.

"We're through, Gary," said Jane, with a toss of her black hair.

"No more for us," said Bill. He was a slender young man with glasses.

Gary looked puzzled. "What's the matter?"

"The phantom horse again," his friend replied. "It came out of the fog last night and frightened us," Jane replied. "Sea gulls or no, we're going home."

"Maybe we can help you," Pam Hollister said, stepping up to Jane. The older girl cast a puzzled

16

glance at Pam, whose eager face looked brightly up at her.

"We've solved mysteries before," Pam went on. "Look, we have a whole family of detectives here."

"Give us a chance," Pete spoke up. "If there's a ghost horse on that island, maybe we can catch him."

"Don't go," Gary urged. "I think we can solve this mystery and paint our sea gulls, too."

"Of course," said Sue. A drop of ice cream was stuck on the tip of her nose, but her tongue would not quite reach it. She used the back of her hand.

Bill and Jane gazed at the children. Then they looked at each other, pursing their lips. With a nod from the girl, they both smiled and said, "All right, we're game if you stay with us. For tonight, anyhow."

"Good," said Gary, and he quickly introduced his new-found friends.

"Are we going to the island now?" asked Holly.

"You are not!" boomed a voice behind them. They turned to see the ferryman standing at the rail of his craft. His cap was pushed back on his bristly gray hair and his thumbs were hooked in his belt. "The *Mermaid* won't sail again till morning."

"Are you the captain?" asked Ricky.

"I am. Captain Jeremiah Wade."

"Where's the crew?" asked Holly.

The captain grinned. "I'm my own crew." Then

he added, "Be on time. We cast off on the dot of nine."

"We'd better tell Indy," Pete said.

"And get rooms for the night," put in Gary. As the gull team hurried off, the Hollisters followed toward the station wagon. Indy had begun to unpack it, and the Snowman had moved his cart onto the dock again. When they neared it, Pete noticed a man strolling a little distance from them. He wore a beret and had a brown beard.

Just then Holly spotted a lone gull wheeling above in the fading light. "Look!" she cried. "A green one!" She flung up her arm toward the bird and the last bit of her ice cream flew off the stick. As the gull swooped toward the ice cream, the white blob landed *smack!* on the man's shoe. He stopped short and looked down.

Holly gasped, then said timidly, "I'm awfully sorry."

"It's nothing," he said, and, whipping out a handkerchief, wiped the polished leather. They could tell by his accent that he was not a native American.

"I am sorry about your ice cream," the stranger added. "I'll get you another one."

"Oh, you don't have to do that," Holly said politely as the man stepped to the wagon. "It wasn't your fault." But the stranger made her a little bow and handed her a snow-stick. Holly beamed and thanked him.

The man smiled at Holly. "So you like sea gulls, do you?"

"We're going to catch them and paint them," Ricky boasted.

"Over there on Nick-Nack Island," piped up Sue.

"Oh," the bearded man asked, "you're going to Wicket-ee-nock?"

Holly bobbed her head, and as they all moved away from the Snowman she began telling the stranger about their plans. He seemed interested and asked many questions.

As the eager youngsters finished talking, a far-away look came to the man's blue eyes and without a word he walked off the pier toward the main street of Cliffport.

"He was a funny duck," Pete said. "I wonder what country he came from?"

As soon as the Hollisters were settled at the motel they gathered in Indy's room while he telephoned Shoreham. After he had told Mr. Hollister of their plan to stay on Wicket-ee-nock, the children took turns talking.

"There's a mystery on the island, Mother," Ricky said importantly. "We may have to stay longer and solve it."

"Well," said Mrs. Hollister, "we won't worry if you do, but don't forget that Daddy and I miss you."

Finally, after Sue had chirped kisses into the phone, Indy hung up and they all went to bed.

19

Early the next morning the travelers were up and eager to cross the channel to the island. Right after breakfast, Holly gave Blackie a bowl of milk, while the other children packed suitcases.

Indy and Emmy bought supplies at a small grocery. When they returned with four large, bulging sacks, Ricky exclaimed, "Yikes! All that food!"

"Better too much than too little," Emmy replied. "It won't go to waste."

Ten minutes later, when they all gathered on the dock, the Snowman was there with his cart. He waved to the children as they watched Indy drive the station wagon onto the ferryboat. With a jingle-jangle and a thump, it went aboard.

The children and Blackie raced onto the deck, followed by Emmy and the gullers. Then the captain untied the ropes, gave three toots on the whistle, and the boat set off toward the island.

The day was bright and windy, and the flag atop the tall mast whipped and snapped in the breeze. But halfway across, the ferry began to list to one side. Captain Wade called to Indy, "Here, grab the wheel! I've got to see what's the trouble."

He hastened below and returned, highly excited. "There's a hole in the boat!" he exclaimed. "We're sinking! Everyone has to bail!"

CHAPTER 3

A Scolding

"YOUNG lady, take the wheel!" ordered the captain. "The men'll have to man the buckets!"

Pam took the huge steering wheel from Indy and kept the boat on a straight course, while Holly and Sue gave her excited directions. At the same time, Pete and Ricky raced to the side of the deck and pulled the canvas cover off a lifeboat. It was old and rickety. "Crickets!" exclaimed Pete, "I hope we don't have to use this!"

Captain Wade, meanwhile, grasped four red buckets hanging in the stern. He quickly formed a bailing brigade. Pails full of sloshing water were handed up from the leaky bottom and tossed over the side.

The boat kept its list, but did not keel over any farther. Pam held the course true, lining up the bow of the ferry with the dock that she could see on Wicket-ee-nock Island.

As they neared it, the captain sprang back to the wheel. "Thanks," he said. With his jaw set grimly, he guided the boat alongside the dock in the shallow water. After Indy had driven the station wagon off the ferry, the men and boys inspected the damage.

"Tarnation!" Captain Wade said. "One of the seams has opened up."

"It looks as if it was done on purpose, too," Pete pointed out. Marks of a chisel were seen along the ripped-open seam a few inches below the water line.

"Why would anyone want to sink my boat?" the skipper asked angrily. In the same breath he added, "I'll repair it right now."

From a locker located in the stern, the captain pulled out some tools and a coil of rope. Then he hammered the rope into the open seam.

"There," he said, "this will get me back to the mainland, anyway."

The Hollisters watched as the ferry started the return journey. When it was about a quarter of the way over, Holly shrieked, "Look! It's sinking again!"

They could see the skipper trying to bail it out, but it was no use. Since there was no one at the wheel, the ferry circled around. Captain Wade hopped into the lifeboat, and they could see him stroking hard toward the opposite shore. Finally the big boat settled into the water with only its flag mast showing above the surface.

"Now we have a real problem!" Emmy said. "With no ferry, we'll have to stay on the island more than one night."

Gary, Bill, and Jane grinned when they heard this. "It's an ill wind that blows no good," Gary said. "That means you can help us catch gulls."

After they had seen Captain Wade land safely at Cliffport, the travelers looked about the island.

"Look! It's sinking again!"

Their car was on a sandy road that ran parallel to the beach. First they drove to the south end to let off the gull catchers at a small grove of pines. Gary said they would tramp through the trees and then across dunes to the nesting rocks to pitch their two tents.

"We'll be down to see you," Pete promised. Then Indy drove north, past the deserted inn and up to the white house. They all got out of the car and walked to the front door, which opened before they reached it. A thin, gray-haired woman, wearing dungarees, stepped out to meet them. "I'm Maude Franklin," she said. "Is there something I can do for you?"

Emmy Roades told of their permission to stay on the island overnight. "But I think we'll have to remain longer," she said, and explained about the ferry boat.

"Stay longer? What was that?" came a voice from inside the house. Out stepped a man with stern, weatherworn features. He wore dungarees, too, and a wide leather belt cinched tightly around his narrow waistline.

"This is my husband, Amos," Mrs. Franklin said.

"We don't like people staying on this island," Mr. Franklin said.

Indy explained there was nothing he could do. "All our belongings are in the station wagon," he said. "We'll be here until the ferry is raised and repaired."

Amos Franklin shook his head and his wife looked annoyed.

"Well, all right," the man said. "But I warn you to stay away from the barn." He pointed to the white building on the promontory.

"Is that where the ghost horse lives?" Sue chirped.

Maude Franklin's face looked pale when she heard this.

"Ghost horse! That's silly. This is private property, that's all." The woman thrust her hands into her pockets uneasily, as if wishing their callers would leave. Sensing this, Emmy said, "Well, come on, children, we'll unpack at the old inn."

On the way back to the station wagon, Pete stopped and Ricky halted beside him. The boys turned to look in the direction of the barn and took a few steps for a better view.

Thump! Thump! The sound drifted lightly to their ears.

"Hey, what was that?" Ricky whispered.

But they did not have time to think about it, for Mrs. Franklin dashed toward them. "Boys, I told you to stay away from the barn!" she cried out.

Pete and Ricky grew red with embarrassment. "I'm sorry," Pete said. "We weren't—"

"Please go away!" Mrs. Franklin exclaimed.

Indy beckoned to the two boys, who sheepishly followed the others into the station wagon.

"I think she's angry with you," Pam said.

"Yikes! We didn't do anything," Ricky said. "But we did hear a funny noise."

"Come on," Emmy said, "your imaginations are working overtime."

Pete and Ricky remained silent as the station wagon approached the old inn and stopped in front of it. The faded red sign hung askew and swung back and forth in the breeze.

"There's one thing I can do, repair that sign," Indy said, stepping out of the car. He looked at the two boys. "Don't take it so hard," he added, "you've been scolded before, haven't you?"

"But we weren't doing anything," Ricky protested.

"Come on," Pam said kindly. "This looks like a spooky old place. Let's forget about the Franklins."

The inn was unpainted and weather-beaten. Weeds grew around the steps which led to the long porch in front of the building. Several boards had fallen through, so the visitors had to pick their way carefully to the front door.

Pete, first inside, saw that plaster had fallen from the parlor ceiling and strips of lath showed through like skeleton ribs.

In the corner stood a cracked potbellied stove. As Holly reached to open it, Emmy said, "Don't touch that! You'll get all full of soot!"

The dining room was no better than the parlor, and the kitchen was worse. The stove and sink had been removed, and all that was left was a rickety table.

But down the hall the travelers found three bedrooms in fairly good condition.

"This place needs to be swept out before we set up our folding cots," Pam said.

Holly found an old push broom and a mop in a corner, and the children took turns sweeping out the bedrooms. Emmy got a clean rag from the glove compartment of the car and wiped the cobwebby windows.

"There," the Indian girl said brightly. "The old Lobster Inn will be livable in no time at all."

Holly shrugged and twirled one of her pigtails. "But where are we going to cook?"

"I saw an old fireplace out front," Pam said.

"Then we can have cookouts every day!" declared Sue.

While the girls swept, Blackie tried to play tag with the broom, but he soon tired and lay down on the porch, where Pete had placed Fluffy's cage. The dog watched as the boys unloaded the station wagon and Indy repaired the lobster sign.

At noon the workers ate a sandwich lunch in front of the inn. When they had finished, Pete opened Fluffy's cage. The sleepy owl fluffed up her feathers and flew out.

"There she goes!" shouted Ricky, but Fluffy landed on the lobster sign and promptly dozed off again.

"She didn't go very far," said Sue with a chuckle.

All afternoon the travelers kept busy sprucing up the Lobster Inn. The cots were set up and made with clean white sheets.

Pam found an old-fashioned pump in back of the inn near a high sand dune. She pumped the handle, and, much to her surprise, clear water squirted out of it at once.

"That's funny," she thought, and carried a pailful into the inn. As she mopped her bedroom floor, she guessed that the boys or Indy had been using the pump and thought no more of it.

Meanwhile, Pete opened the tool kit in the back of the station wagon. He and Ricky scrounged about for some nails, and the three menfolk repaired a loose shutter, a few dangling boards, and a hole in the front steps.

At suppertime Emmy opened a few cans and prepared a delicious meal on the outdoor grill. Then, as the big red sun was sinking, Fluffy suddenly flew off the sign.

"Come back!" Sue called.

"Let her go," Pete said. "Fluffy is going to forage for food."

"Like what?"

"A mouse maybe. That's what owls eat."

"Ugh! I'm glad I'm not an owl," said Holly as she stood watching the hot coals glow in the fireplace.

Half an hour later, when the bird had not returned, Sue became worried.

"When is Fluffy coming back?" she asked Pete.

"Probably never," he replied. Sue's eyes filled with tears. "You mustn't feel bad," he went on kindly. "She's really a wild bird, you know. She wants to be free."

"But I didn't even say good-by," said Sue as the tears spilled over.

"I'll tell you what, honey." Pam spoke up quickly. "We'll go for a walk and if we see Fluffy, you can wave to her." Pam dried the little girl's eyes with a tissue, took her by the hand, and set out behind the inn.

"Here, Fluffy, Fluffy!" Sue called out as they approached a high sand hill.

Just then Pam stopped and gasped. In the dusk she could see the dark figure of a man crawling up the dune.

CHAPTER 4

Pete's Prize

PAM strained her eyes to see who the prowler was. But the man slithered over the top of the dune and disappeared down the other side.

The girl hesitated for a moment; then, holding Sue's hand tightly, she raced over and scrambled up the sandy slope to the spot where the prowler had vanished. Some distance below Pam saw footprints, which she followed to the bottom of the dune.

There the tracks led toward the ocean side of the island, a quarter of a mile distant. The sisters could hear the waves breaking onto the sandy shore.

Darkness was now falling rapidly, and Pam hesitated to follow the footprints farther. With the wind blowing her fluffy hair, she turned and trudged back toward the Lobster Inn with Sue. On the way she wondered who the intruder could be. The man with the beret, perhaps? The person who had asked so many questions of the Hollisters the night before?

When the two girls reached the inn, Pam told of trailing the stranger.

"Crickets!" Pete said. "Let's follow those tracks first thing in the morning, Pam."

Emmy had bought a dozen candles, so the children prepared for bed in the soft shimmering light. When the tiny flames had been snuffed, the travelers fell fast asleep.

Pete had set his mind to wake up early. His eyes fluttered open in the gray light of dawn. He dressed quickly, then quietly awakened Pam. Together they tiptoed from the inn, climbed up the sand dune and down the other side.

"See," Pam said. "The tracks are still clear."

From the length of the stride, Pete reasoned that the stranger had been running. The children followed the trail to the ocean shore. There the footprints disappeared in the surf.

Pete looked disappointed. "Whoever it was went right into the ocean," he said.

"Perhaps he walked along in the surf for a while to hide his tracks," Pam suggested.

The children trudged up the beach, then down, but could find no further trail of the fugitive.

By the time they made their way back to the inn, Ricky had already lighted a cheery fire for a breakfast cookout.

Sue came running to meet them. "Look!" she cried. "Fluffy's back!" She pointed to the lobster sign. There sat the owl with her eyes shut.

Pete chuckled. "I've heard of a homing pigeon, but never a homing owl."

"This one must be different," Pam said, smiling at Sue's happy look.

After a hearty meal of scrambled eggs, toast, and

hot chocolate, Indy said, "I think Emmy, Sue, and I should visit the Franklins to ask about that prowler."

"Do you suppose it could have been Mr. Franklin?" asked Ricky.

"I doubt that," came the reply, "but I think we'd better check anyhow."

"Then the rest of us can go catch sea gulls!" Ricky said hopefully.

"Okay," replied Indy. "You be in charge, Pete, and take care on those rocky shores."

Carrying sandwich lunches, the four older children ran along the beach with Blackie toward the southern tip of Wicket-ee-nock. After passing through the cool pine grove they came out onto sunny dunes again. The island was narrower here and the children could see both shores at once. In the distance Pete spied two orange tents. Beyond them the sand gradually gave way to rocks. There the youngsters could make out Gary, Bill, and Jane setting gull traps.

"Oh, look!" exclaimed Holly. "Here's a nest!"

In it were three small eggs, which Blackie barked at.

"Yikes, there's another one over there!" Ricky said, pointing.

Overhead, several gulls wheeled and cried shrilly at the children.

"We'd better not touch any eggs," Pam said as they made their way toward the tents.

Ricky lingered behind a moment, then joined

the others as they continued to count the eggs in the nests. Some had two, others three.

When the children neared the gullers' camp, Ricky suddenly cried out, "Oh, look! Here's a nest with six eggs in it!"

Jane, who had just finished setting a trap, looked up, surprised. "Six eggs?" she asked. "Where?"

Dressed in shorts and a shirt, Jane sprang over the rocks to where Ricky stood. In the nest at the boy's feet were six eggs. "You can't play a trick like that on me," Jane said.

"What do you mean?" asked Ricky with a look of innocence on his face.

"Sea gulls have no more than three eggs in a nest," she replied.

"That's right," said Bill as he and Gary walked over.

Ricky's ears became red.

"You've played a trick," Pam said, "else why are your ears so pink?"

The redhead admitted he had carried three eggs from a nest farther along the ridge.

"Then go put them back," Jane said kindly.

As Ricky did this, Jane showed the girls her living quarters.

"Bill and I stay in the other tent," Gary said. "Do you want to peek inside, Pete?"

The boy pulled back the tent flap to see two neat sleeping bags, along with other camping gear inside the tent.

"Yikes!" said Ricky, hurrying back. "It must be great to live outdoors like this."

"So far so good," Gary said with a shrug. Pete realized that the older boy was purposely saying nothing about the ghost horse story.

"Come on," Bill said. "Let's catch sea gulls."

"May we help you?" Pete asked.

Gary replied that all the net traps had been set. "But you boys can use this fish line if you want."

After he had instructed Pete what to do, the two brothers traipsed off to find a gull nest. Before they had gone very far, they heard Holly cry out with delight as a bird was caught in one of the net traps. Jane lifted out the captive and the girls prepared to paint it.

"Come on, Pete," Ricky said. "Let's catch a sea gull of our own so we can paint it, too."

Pete made a loop in the fish line and spread the noose about the edge of a nest as he had been instructed. Then, carefully paying out line, the boys retreated along the ledge and lay down on their stomachs to await the arrival of the gulls.

Many birds wheeled overhead but none of them landed on the nest. As the boys waited, Blackie scrambled over the rocks to their side.

Just then a sea gull poised over the nest and started to land on it.

As Ricky jerked the line, Blackie barked. With a great flapping of wings the gull took off again and the noose closed on thin air.

"Oh, yikes!" Ricky exclaimed. "Blackie, be

quiet! How are we going to catch any birds with you around?"

The dog put his head between his paws and lay quietly while Pete went out to reset the noose. This time the older boy took the pole in his hands and waited patiently.

The same gull soared overhead and, seeing no movement from the boys, descended again. As its feet touched down, Pete yanked on the fish pole. The noose tightened around the gull's legs and off it soared into the air.

"Grab it! Hold it!" Ricky shouted to his brother.

"I'm doing the best I can!" Pete said as the line was pulled out and the reel spun.

"Pull him in, Pete!" Ricky shouted as the gull kept struggling upward.

"Crickets!" said his brother. "This is bigger than the biggest fish I ever caught!"

With the gull flapping mightily, Pete started to reel in the long line. Gradually, the bird fluttered lower and lower.

"Yikes, we got him!" Ricky cried out gleefully.

As the big gull came head high, the redhead grabbed its legs. The bird pecked at the boy's hands, but Ricky held on stoutly.

"We caught one!" Pete shouted.

"Bring him over, we'll paint him," Bill called back.

Proudly the boys scrambled over the rocks with their captive. They walked to Jane's tent, where

"Pull him in, Pete!"

Pam and Holly had just finished painting their gull with red dye from a white porcelain pail.

"Good catch," Bill praised Pete. "Do you want to color this one yourselves?"

"Sure," Ricky replied. "If the girls can, we can too!"

"But you must be careful," Pam said, "not to get any paint in the bird's eyes." She handed her younger brother a piece of tissue, saying, "Put this over its head."

Pete held the captive's feet and Ricky the neck, covering its head with the paper. Then Pete took the paintbrush Pam handed him and started to daub the gull's feathers.

Ricky grinned with delight. "I know an old alley cat in Shoreham I'd like to paint!" the boy said impishly as Pete stroked a brushful of dye onto the bird's neck. "Look out, you're getting it on my fingers," Ricky added.

As Pete finished coloring the gull, he said, "Now where do we dry these critters?"

Pam pointed across the dune to a large cage made of chicken wire. The other red sea gull was already in it. Pete carried his to the enclosure, opened the top, and dropped the bird inside.

"They'll dry in two hours," Jane said. "Then we release them."

The girl went on to explain that if you let the sea gulls go immediately, they would head directly into the surf and wash the paint off their feathers.

Before the morning was over, seven gulls were captured, painted, and released.

"You Hollisters are a big help," Gary declared.

After they had eaten their sandwiches, the afternoon sped by and shortly before five o'clock the children heard the horn of their station wagon.

"Emmy wants us for supper," Pam said.

"Come back and visit us later," Jane invited as the children set off.

When they reached the inn, Pete asked, "Indy, did you find out who that prowler was last night?"

"The Franklins didn't seem to know anything about him," came the reply. "We'd better keep our eyes open. Did you catch any gulls?"

While they ate supper, the youngsters told about their day's adventures. As Emmy passed out candy bars for dessert, Fluffy roused herself, spread her wings, and flew off to get her evening meal. Sue watched her go, then said, "I want to see Jane's tent."

"Okay, I'll take you there," Ricky volunteered.

It was decided that Emmy, Indy, Sue, and Blackie should accompany Holly and Ricky to the gullers' camp. Pete and Pam, meanwhile, would walk to the place where they had seen the footprints that morning.

When Pete and Pam reached the shore, they looked up and down. No one was in sight. The prints had been washed away.

"Where do you suppose the fellow went after he walked into the water?" Pam asked.

"He may have waded out to a boat," Pete replied.

Some distance up the beach the children could see the jagged rocks of the cliff with the barn on top.

At Pam's suggestion, they walked to the foot of the sea cliff, where a great jumble of boulders extended into the pounding surf.

"Crickets, you can't get past here when the tide is high," Pete noted. He nearly had to shout for his sister to hear him. Just then Pam glanced up at the cliff, and her mouth fell open.

"What's the matter?" Pete asked, looking up.

A man stood among the rocks. He had his hands cupped to his mouth and was shouting at them.

"Can you hear what he's saying?" Pete cried.

"No!"

The fellow took his hands from his face and waved the children away from the boulders.

"It's the man with the beard!" Pete cried.

CHAPTER 5

Hoofbeats on the Sand

"WHAT do you want?" Pete called up to the man standing on the rocks above them. The stranger waved his hand once more before turning to scramble over the crags and disappear into the deep shadows.

"What do we do now?" Pam asked.

"Maybe the Franklins know something about that fellow," her brother replied. "Come on. Let's go to their house and ask them."

"But it's getting late."

"Emmy and the rest won't worry about us," Pete said. "We're old enough to take care of ourselves."

Pete knew that climbing the craggy cliff at this hour would be too dangerous. So he and Pam walked back along the damp, sandy beach to a spot where the island leveled off. Then they headed west, making a beeline through some scrubby growth toward the opposite side of Wicket-ee-nock.

Reaching the beach there, they turned north on the road and soon were trotting up the path that led to the Franklins' home. Behind it on the promontory, the white barn looked ghostly in the twilight. Pete and Pam glanced around quickly, but there was no sign of the peculiar stranger.

Pete knocked on the door. Then he knocked

again. After a long wait the door opened and Mrs. Franklin stood before them.

"We'd like to talk to you," Pete said.

The woman smiled faintly, but did not invite them inside. Instead she stepped out, closing the door behind her.

"Now what is it that's bothering you children?"

"There seems to be a mystery here," Pam said, and told Mrs. Franklin about the man who had waved at them.

"Do you know him?" Pete asked.

"Why—why no," came the reply.

"Well, he disappeared up in those rocks behind your barn," Pete said. "We thought perhaps he worked for you or something."

The woman shot a frightened look toward the barn. "Oh, dear," she said softly, but quickly regained her composure.

"Mrs. Franklin," Pam asked kindly, "what do you and your husband do for a living on Wicket-ee-nock Island?"

Even in the fading evening light, Pam noticed that Mrs. Franklin looked suddenly drawn. She fidgeted with her handkerchief. Then, with a shake of her head, she said, "Please children, don't ask me that question."

"Crickets! We didn't mean to shake you up, Mrs. Franklin," Pete said. "Are you in some kind of trouble?"

"No, it's not that!" The woman turned toward the door, then swung about quickly. "All I can tell you is that my husband and I are engaged on a secret job." Her voice was husky as she wished them good night. Then she slipped into her home and closed the door quietly behind her.

"That poor woman," Pam said as she and Pete retraced their steps toward the shore. "I'm sorry we even asked her about that man."

"I'll bet there's a bigger mystery going on here than we thought," Pete said. Then he snapped his fingers. "Pam! Do you suppose the fellow we saw was Mr. Franklin in disguise?"

The girl stopped for a moment to empty the sand from her shoes. "I don't think so. Why would he disguise himself?"

"That's right," her brother agreed as they set off again. "There doesn't seem to be any reason."

A pale moon hung high in the sky, providing some light for the youngsters as they neared the Lobster Inn.

"The others must be back by this time," Pete commented as he broke into a jog.

"I think so," Pam replied. "Look, I see some lights flickering in the inn." Now both children ran fast, kicking up little spurts of sand behind them.

"Ricky, Holly, we're back!" Pete called out.

An instant later the lights went out.

"They're going to play a joke on us," Pam said and cried out, "We know you're there! You can't fool us!"

42

Suddenly two figures, crouching low, ran out of the inn and made for the shore.

Pete and Pam stopped short. "That's not Ricky and Holly!" exclaimed Pam.

Moments later they heard a motor cough to life and saw a small boat head across the channel toward the mainland.

"Crickets!" Pete blurted. "Somebody's been spying on us."

They raced for the inn and dashed in the front door. Pete felt about until he found a match on the hall table and lighted a candle. They went straight to Pam and Holly's room.

"Oh dear!" Pam exclaimed as the tiny glow revealed opened suitcases and clothes strewn about.

"The place has been ransacked!" Pete said.

Quickly they checked the other bedrooms. All three were topsy-turvy.

As they went out into the hall again, happy voices sounded from outside and the other travelers came in.

"We've been robbed!" Pete told them.

"By the ghost horse?" Sue asked in a slow sleepy voice.

"We're not fooling," Pam said. "Look at the bedrooms!"

Quickly the travelers separated to check on their personal belongings. In a short time they met in Emmy and Sue's room. Nothing had been taken from it.

"That's not Ricky and Holly!" exclaimed Pam.

"Pete and I aren't missing anything," Indy reported.

"All of our stuff was there, too," Holly said. "They couldn't have been real burglars."

"They were looking for something, that's for sure," Ricky said, scratching his red head.

"Oh, look!" Emmy exclaimed as she held a candle toward her cot. A small book lay on it face down and open. "Somebody's disturbed my diary."

Holly held her candle close to the book as Emmy examined it. None of the pages was missing.

"But see here," Emmy said, and pointed to a smudged thumbmark on the page where she had written about leaving from Shoreham with the Hollisters.

"Maybe the crooks wanted to find out who we are," Pete suggested.

"Then that rules out the man with the beard," Pam commented. "He knows all about us."

"But not about Emmy," Pete argued. He and Pam then told of seeing the stranger on the cliff.

"Well," Indy said, "we can't do anything tonight. Let's get this place shipshape and tumble in."

Ricky was first to skin into his pajamas and climb between the cool sheets of his cot. Pete settled down quickly beside him, but not for long. First, Blackie growled and the two boys sat up and listened.

"Do you suppose someone's prowling around?" whispered Ricky.

"Shhh. Listen."

In the distance came the sound of hoofbeats.

"The ghost horse!" Ricky exclaimed, bounding to his feet.

"Do you hear that noise?" Pam called out from the next room.

Soon the hall was aglow with candlelight. Everybody was awake, listening to the hoofbeats.

Indy hastened outside, dropped to the ground, and pressed his ear against the sand.

"What do you hear, Indy?" Ricky asked.

"That's a real horse, not a ghost," the Indian said, rising to his feet. "In fact, there are two horses."

"What color are they?" asked Sue, rubbing her eyes with the back of her chubby fists.

The chuckles that followed relieved the tension and Indy said, "Back to bed, all of you. There's nothing to fear. We'll look for hoofprints in the morning."

Emmy made everyone eat breakfast before they went out to search for the horses' tracks. Then they all headed up the channel beach in the direction from which the sound had come.

Ricky ranged ahead like a hound-dog, his head low and his arms dangling at his side. Suddenly the redhead shouted, "Here they are!"

When the others caught up they saw a jumble of deep hoofprints in the sand.

"This is where they turned around," said Indy, then pointed up the beach. "You can see their prints coming and going."

"Tell us about them," said Ricky. "What kind of horses they were and all that."

"They were large heavy animals," Indy replied.

"But Gary told us the ghost horse was little," said Holly, puzzled.

The searchers followed the trail past the dock where the tracks turned inland. After a short time sand gave way to bare rock and there the prints vanished.

Disappointed, the travelers returned to the Lobster Inn, where Fluffy was once again napping on the sign.

Before setting off to visit the gullers, everyone helped to tidy the place. As Pam smoothed the sheets on her cot, Holly called out that someone was rowing toward the shore.

The young detectives hurried out to meet the new arrival, with Blackie frisking along beside them. The man, his back to them as he rowed, gave one final pull on the oars, then stepped from the boat and drew it up on the sand. He was a scraggly fellow with tattered dungarees and a faded blue shirt. His eyelids drooped as if he were about to fall asleep.

"Hello there," Pete said. "Are you looking for us?"

The man eyed Blackie uneasily and said, "I have something for Emily Roades."

47

"Oh, Emmy!" Holly called, running back to the house. "There's someone wants to see you!"

Emmy hastened out with Indy at her side. The sleepy-looking stranger handed her a yellow envelope. "It's a telegram," he said.

As Emmy tore it open, the courier quickly returned to his boat, pushed it into the water, hopped in, and bent to his oars again. Hardly noticing this, Emmy scanned the telegram. "Oh, goodness gracious!" she exclaimed.

"Yikes! What's the matter?" Ricky asked.

Emmy looked sad and puzzled as she read: "Bring children home at once. Signed Mrs. Hollister."

Suddenly there was not a smile on any of the five young faces.

CHAPTER 6

Funny Little Chicks

"You mean we have to go home right away without solving the mystery?" Ricky asked glumly as he kicked the sand.

"But we can't get our car to the mainland," protested Pete. He gazed out at the ferryboat mast, still sticking up in the middle of the channel.

Pam shook her head and took the telegram from Emmy. "This doesn't sound like Mother," she said. "She wouldn't send you such a rude order, Emmy."

"People always talk short in telegrams," said Ricky, "because each word costs money."

"Pam's right," Pete chimed in. "I think Mother would have explained more."

"And she never signs herself *Mrs.* Hollister," Pam went on. "It's not proper."

Ricky's eyes lit up. "Maybe the telegram's a phony!"

"I'll bet it is," Pete declared. "The prowlers, whoever they are, found our address in Emmy's diary. Then they called the telegraph office in Cliffport, and pretended to be in Shoreham."

"You may be right," Indy agreed. "We'll check on the telegram as soon as we can get to the mainland." He warned the children that they must be extremely cautious. "Someone wants us off Wicket-ee-nock."

"Maybe they're doing something illegal, like smuggling," Pete suggested.

"That's right!" Ricky spoke up. "The man on the cliff might have been signaling to a ship."

"And the stuff may be stored in the white barn," Holly added.

Although the idea seemed to be a wild one, Pam remembered the secrecy surrounding the Franklins. The thought occurred to her that Mr. Franklin might have had the telegram sent.

Holly and Ricky exchanged glances. If they could only see what was inside that white barn!

The Hollisters mulled over the mystery as they trudged toward the gullers' camp. The sand was hot beneath their bare feet and the ocean was sparkling blue.

"Yikes," said Ricky, swinging his shoes, "I want to go swimming."

"It's a good thing we wore our bathing suits under our shorts," Holly remarked as they rounded a dune. Then she exclaimed, "Oh, look!"

A short distance ahead they saw Jane struggling to paint a large gull. Wisps of hair were blowing in her face and the bird was flapping wildly.

"Help!" she called, laughing, as the children ran to her aid. Soon the captive was painted and put in a pen to dry.

"There," Jane said as the bright red gull

"Help!"

stretched its wings and strutted about. "I've painted as many as the boys have caught."

"Then we'll help them catch more," Pete declared with a grin. He and Ricky joined Bill and Gary as the older boys went over the rocks to set gull nets.

"Have you taken a good look at the birds on their nests?" asked Jane as she pulled off her rubber gloves.

"No," Pam replied.

"Well, come with me and we'll do it," Jane said, taking Sue by the hand.

"But I'm going to put on my shoes," said Holly. "The sand's too hot."

As they walked toward the tip of the island Pam told their friend all that happened the night before. Before long they scrambled up a sandy slope to the low rocky ramparts where the gulls had built their nests. Some of the birds flew off in alarm as the girls lay down and rested their elbows on the warm sand.

"Lie very still," Jane cautioned, "and watch."

Several gulls circled overhead, gliding and dipping down toward the nests. One held a long piece of straw in its beak. As it neared the ground, it made a mewing noise and the straw fell out.

"If you carry things in your mouth," Jane said with a chuckle, "you shouldn't talk!"

"Oh, look at that big bird!" Pam exclaimed, glancing up.

"I'll bet it's an eagle," said Holly.

Jane told them that it was a black-backed gull. "It weighs three pounds while the others weigh only two."

"What a large wingspread it has," Pam remarked, shading her eyes and gazing at the soaring creature.

"But those big fellows are dangerous," Jane said. "When they peck people it really hurts!"

As the girls lay quietly in the sunshine the birds they had disturbed gradually returned to the rocks.

"Now look carefully," Jane said softly, and motioned to a nest not far from them. Inside were several grayish, speckled, downy chicks.

"Aren't they cute!" said Sue in a tiny voice. Two gulls strutted nearby, cocking their heads occasionally toward the nest. The young birds stretched and yawned. One awkwardly lost its balance and fell over. Holly giggled as the bird stood up again.

Then the mother bird came with food in her beak. At once the chicks began to peck at her bill, spreading their little wings and uttering squeaking noises.

After the young ones were fed, they fell asleep and the mother bird spread her wings over them.

As Jane showed the girls another nest of babies, Holly moved suddenly to slap a fly biting her leg. This frightened the two parent gulls. They rose in the air giving a hoarse cry of *Hahaha!*

"That's the alarm call to the young," Jane explained quietly. As she spoke, the gull chicks jumped out of the nest and ran into the shade of Holly's body and crouched down.

"They're looking for shelter," Jane said with a smile. "They don't know that we're the cause of alarm."

"May I pick them up?" asked Holly.

"Better not," Jane advised, eying the parent birds. "No use upsetting them any more."

Holly got carefully to her feet, and instantly the chicks began to peck at her red sandals.

As she and Pam laughed, the other gulls rose from their nests calling hoarsely.

"When you hear that cry," Jane went on, "you know something has disturbed the birds."

On the way back to camp she explained that gulls respond to the color red. "Did you see the way the babies pecked at the mother's beak?" she asked. "They're attracted by a little red mark on it. When they peck toward that spot, the mother pops a morsel of food in their mouths."

"I'm hungry too," Sue spoke up. "Is there anything red I can eat?"

Jane laughed and said indeed there was. When they reached her tent she sliced several ripe red tomatoes and, adding lettuce, made sandwiches for lunch.

"Yummy," said Holly. "I like lots of mayonnaise on mine."

Ricky, shouting at the top of his lungs, returned twenty minutes later with a sea gull. The other boys were right behind him. Jane and Pam hastened outside to paint the bird. When they returned to the tent Sue was sound asleep, with Holly dozing beside her.

Jane put her finger to her lips and beckoned the boys aside. "The gull watching has worn them out," she said. "Do you want some lunch?"

"We've had it already," Ricky replied. "We came back early and went out again."

"Can we go exploring now?" Pete asked.

"If someone stays near the tents," Jane replied with a glance toward the sleepers.

"Bill and I'll be working here," Gary said. "Where do you want to go?"

"The place we saw that man waving to us last night," Pete replied.

He and Pam, with Jane and Ricky, trotted along the beach. When they reached the cliff, the tide was in and large waves were booming onto the rocks. Suddenly Pam pointed. "There's the spot!" They could see now that the fellow had been perched high atop giant caverns. They loomed like dark hollow eyes part way up the cliff.

"Goodness, that would be scary enough to enter even at low tide," Jane said with a twinkle. Now it was impossible to go into the cave mouths, which were gurgling and frothing as the wave tops hit them.

Unable to explore the crags, the four turned back.

As they approached the camp, they saw Holly and Sue playing in the surf while Bill and Gary swam nearby. With a whoop Ricky broke into a run and five minutes later everyone was in the water.

It was late afternoon when the Hollisters finally came out to dry in the sun. Just as they were putting on their shorts and tops, Blackie dashed around a dune, barking joyfully. Right behind him were Emmy and Indy, who was carrying a large cardboard carton.

"How about a cookout?" Emmy asked and was answered by a chorus of happy yeses.

The long stretch of beach on both sides of the island lay deserted as Pete built a campfire. His sisters, meanwhile, went into Jane's tent to put on warmer clothes, which Emmy had brought.

Later, when the frankfurters sizzled and their juice burst out, Pam wished that all her friends in Shoreham might be enjoying the picnic with them that evening.

After the sun had set and the fire had burned low, heavy clouds rolled in from the west. Emmy said it was time to return to the inn. Jane could tell by the look in Pam's eyes that she wished to remain overnight in the tent.

"May Pam stay with me?" Jane asked Emmy.

"Yes, me too," Holly said.

"And me," chimed in Sue.

"Pam may if she likes," Emmy replied. "As for you other two scamps, who's going to keep me company tonight?"

Holly and Sue both hugged Emmy at the same

time. Then Gary spoke up. "Could Pete stay with Bill and me?" When Indy nodded Yes, Ricky looked disappointed, but was assured that he would have a chance later on.

After the others had gone, Pete, Pam, and the gull team huddled around the fire. The clouds settled lower, and soon a white fog began to roll in off the sea.

"Let's not tell ghost stories now," Pam said, glancing uneasily into the heavy mist.

Bill tried to laugh, but he was not very good at it. He gulped. "This would be a good night for the—the—"

As he spoke, the quiet beat of hoofs came to their ears. Then the head of a white horse suddenly appeared out of the mist. The embers of the campfire cast a flickering light over the beast. Pam gasped. In the middle of the horse's forehead was a long, cone-shaped horn!

CHAPTER 7

A Voice in the Fog

AT THE sight of the ghostly horse, Pam and Jane screamed. This frightened the strange beast, which disappeared into the fog.

"Let's follow it!" Pete cried out.

Bill and Gary dashed into their tent for flashlights. But these made only white glowing patches in the thick mist. The pursuers went as fast as they could, always fearful that the ghostly horse head might show itself again any moment.

A set of small hoofprints led directly to the water's edge. But by the time Bill and Gary held their lights close to the damp sand, the waves already had begun to wash out the marks.

The young people listened. All was quiet. Talking in whispers, they returned to their tents.

Whose horse was it and where was it kept?

"That horn must be a phony," Pete said.

Bill recalled an ancient story about a unicorn. "That was a mythological horse," he explained, "with a horn in the middle of its head."

By now Pam had begun to shiver in the damp night air. She was glad to crawl into the extra sleeping bag in Jane's tent. "I'm glad the excitement is all over for tonight," she said with a sigh, and fell fast asleep.

Pam woke with a start. Overhead she saw the

Pam and Jane screamed.

orange side of the tent and heard men's voices in the distance. "Jane, what's that?"

Her companion sat up and lifted the tent flap. It was daylight and still foggy. As the men's voices continued, the girls hurriedly dressed. The boys had done the same and, following the sound of the waves, they all made their way toward the water's edge.

"Be careful," whispered Bill. "There's an old anchor sticking up out of the sand near here. Don't trip over it."

"There must be somebody in a boat out there," Pete said.

"We're safe as long as the fog lasts," Jane said, then added, "Wait here. I have an idea." Tugging at Pam's arm, she found the way back to their tent.

"What are you going to do?" Pam asked.

"Just this." Jane handed her a paintbrush and took one herself. Quickly she poured red paint into a bucket, which she carried to where the boys stood. "If anyone wants to hurt us, they're going to get this!" Jane declared, dipping her brush into the crimson dye. The boys chuckled.

The grim look on Jane's face suddenly turned to surprise as a gust of wind cleared away the mist.

"Well, I'll be a purple sea gull!" exclaimed Gary. Not far offshore a small launch rocked on a sand bar. A man stood near the cabin waving his hand. "Help! I need help!"

"Who else is with you?" Pete called cautiously.

"Nobody."

"We heard voices."

"That was my radio," came the reply. The man continued. "I'm delivering this boat down the coast. It has no anchor. Could you throw me a rope so it won't drift off? I want to come ashore."

Bill disappeared and in a moment returned with a long coil of rope. He fastened one end to the half-buried anchor, then flung the coil far out. The man caught the other end in mid-air and tied it to his boat. Then he slid into the water, making his way hand over hand toward the beach.

"He looks awful," Jane whispered to Pam as the fellow waded ashore. From his dirty sneakers to his faded yellow T-shirt, the man was slovenly. His straw-colored hair grew down over his ears, and his pale blue eyes looked at the children through narrow slits. He gave a thin smile.

"Campers, eh?" he asked, cocking his head. "Where's your mom and pop?"

"We work for the Audubon Society," Bill replied.

The sailor's eyes slid to rest on the paint bucket. "Oh, I see," he said, "gull painters. Then there must be gull eggs around here."

Without another word, he strode along the beach a way, bent down, and soon returned with a dozen sea-gull eggs in his large hands.

"You'd better put those back," ordered Gary.

Bill stepped angrily toward the man, but Jane

61

caught her brother's arm. "Please don't start anything," she begged. "The children might get hurt."

The stranger paid no attention, but walked to their campfire. Before they could say a word, he had broken the eggs into a skillet. The embers from the evening before still glowed, providing heat to fry the eggs. The intruder found a spoon nearby, wiped it on his trousers, and greedily gobbled his illegal breakfast.

"Pete, what'll we do?" Pam whispered to her brother.

"Just let him go, I guess."

The man overheard the remarks and, without turning his head, he moved his eyes toward the Hollisters. "You'd better get off this island," he said. "It's not healthy."

As the others stood watching the unwanted guest, Pam strolled quietly back to the old anchor where Jane had left the red paint and brush. Quickly Pam daubed dye on the rope, then returned to the campfire.

By this time the tide had come in a little, freeing the boat from the sand bar. When the man had bolted the last of the eggs, he tossed down the spoon and with long strides marched to the anchor.

He picked up the rope and coiled it in his hands, drawing his boat closer to shore. "Thanks for the breakfast," he said sarcastically, and thrashed through the shallow water to the craft. "And thanks for the rope, too," he called. "Just what I need!"

The young people watched with relief while he hoisted himself aboard and started the motor. As the boat headed down the coastline, Pam noticed that the name on the side was *The Witch*.

Bill threw up his hands and exclaimed, "All in the life of a gull painter!"

"Why did you color the rope?" asked Jane. "I saw you do it, but I don't think anyone else did."

"I had a hunch he might take it," replied Pam, "and Daddy always says, 'Give someone enough rope and he'll catch himself.'"

"I hope we meet that fellow again," Gary declared. "I'd like to teach him a lesson."

"I'll help you," said Bill. "He knows well enough that it's against the law to destroy sea-gull eggs!"

After a breakfast of bacon and toast and water from thermos jugs, Pete and Pam helped the gullers tidy the tents before starting back to Lobster Inn.

"Come again soon," Bill called out as they waved good-by. "Don't forget to tell Indy about our visitor."

"Do you think that man has something to do with the mystery?" Pam asked as she walked along the sand beside her brother.

Pete shrugged. "Maybe. He warned us to get off the island."

"Yes," Pam said, "and it's funny he should run onto the sand bar so near the place we saw the ghost horse." They puzzled over the mystery until they neared the inn. Suddenly Pam pointed ahead and said, "Look, they're running to meet us!"

Pete shaded his eyes from the morning sun. He saw Ricky, Holly, and Blackie racing pell-mell behind another person.

"That doesn't look like Indy," Pete declared, then added, "Crickets! It's not! Ricky and Holly are chasing someone!"

As the three runners drew closer, Pam exclaimed, "It's that skinny man who delivered the telegram!"

"They're trying to catch him!" Pete cried. "Hey! Stop there!" But the thin man paid no attention as he plowed toward Pete and Pam with Blackie yapping at his heels. Just then Indy appeared, running hard behind the two younger Hollisters. "Catch him, hold him!" he sang out.

Pete dived at the tattered pants legs of the fugitive. The two crashed down and rolled over and over on the sand.

CHAPTER 8

The Mystery Barn

As PETE struggled to keep the man down, Blackie bounded over and licked the fellow's face.

"Help!" spluttered the scraggly man. "Call off the dog!"

Pam collared Blackie and pulled him to her side as Indy raced up. He and Pete helped the captive to his feet.

"Who are you?" the boy asked.

"And why are you running away?" Indy demanded.

The man's eyes were wide with fright as the spaniel strained toward him, wagging his tail.

"The dog was chasing me," he said.

"He was only playing," Holly spoke up.

"And all we wanted was to ask you about that telegram," Ricky added.

"I don't know anything about it," the fellow replied. "I only delivered it." He identified himself as Sleepy Sam, the clam digger. "I don't go around hurting people," he said, looking reproachfully at Pete.

"If I hurt you, I'm sorry," the boy apologized. He explained that there were so many mysterious goings on that he had thought perhaps Sleepy Sam was in league with their enemies.

The man replied that he only delivered a tele-

65

gram occasionally or did odd jobs in Cliffport and dug for clams. "There's a good spot right near the old inn," he said in a happier tone of voice.

"We're sorry we chased you," Holly said, and added quickly, "May we help you dig clams?"

Sleepy Sam nodded with a shy grin and turned to Indy. "That all right with you?"

"Okay," Indy said. "But before you go, can you tell us anything about the telegram? It was a fake."

"Honest," Sam protested, crossing his heart with a bony finger. "I got it from the telegraph clerk in Cliffport."

Pete and Indy nodded, satisfied with Sleepy Sam's honesty. Then they all walked along the shore with Pam holding Blackie firmly in check. She, Pete, and Indy stopped at the inn, while Holly and Ricky continued on with the clam digger. A short distance up the beach they saw a small boat dragged onto the sand. Next to it was a bucket partly filled with clams.

Sleepy Sam reached into the boat for an extra digging fork, which he gave to Ricky. He also pulled out a battered straw hat which he set on Holly's head.

The pigtailed girl thanked him, and ran up and down the beach making the water splash beneath her bare feet.

Ricky and Sleepy Sam busied themselves digging. Clam after clam was dropped into the bucket. In a while Holly came over to watch them.

"Are you really sleepy?" she asked the clam digger.

The man turned to her with droopy eyelids. "I guess I only look that way," he replied, adding that he always got up very early in the morning.

"Oh," Holly said. "Have you lived here very long?"

"All my life," replied Sleepy Sam. "Even when I was little I used to come over here and dig for clams."

"You mean you're a native?" asked Ricky as he squeezed some sand between his toes.

Sleepy Sam nodded.

"Then you know all about Wicket-ee-nock, don't you?" asked Ricky.

When Sam replied that he did, Ricky asked if he would help them solve their mystery.

"About the ghost horse?" the man said. "No, I don't care to deal with spooks."

"Oh, it's just somebody's old horse that got lost," Holly said. She stamped up and down the beach saying, "Wicket-ee-nick, Wicket-ee-nock, the ghost horse lives on the big fat rock."

Sleepy Sam cast a fearful look at the white barn in the distance.

Holly giggled. "Don't worry. I just made that up." Then she splashed up and down again, singing, "Wicket-ee-nick, Wicket-ee-nock, the ghost horse lives on the big fat rock!"

As Ricky dug more clams, the sun beat down on his unprotected head. This made his gingersnap freckles stand out greenish on his pink nose.

"You've had enough sun," Sleepy Sam said. "Besides, I have enough clams. I'd better get back to Cliffport."

Holly returned the straw hat and the man filled the youngsters' hands with clams, suggesting that Emmy make them broth. They thanked him and hurried back to the inn. When they neared the porch, they saw Sue in shorts and a striped shirt running about with arms outstretched toward Fluffy, who swooped over her head.

"Sue'll never catch that owl," Ricky remarked as the bird and his sister disappeared around the other side of the inn.

"Emmy, we have clams for broth!" Holly called as she stepped onto the porch.

"That's fine," said Emmy as she came outside. She was carrying a pot into which the children put the shellfish.

After they had been washed thoroughly, Emmy put a little water in the bottom of the pan and set it on the open fireplace. "Fresh clam broth tastes wonderful," she said. "We'll have it with sandwiches."

While Ricky and Holly were waiting for lunch, Pete and Pam came back from a walk. They sat with the younger children on the porch steps and told them about seeing the ghost horse the night before. Indy and Emmy had heard the story while the younger children were clam digging.

"Weren't you scared?" asked Holly.

"A little," her sister admitted.

"I just hope I'm there the next time it comes," Ricky declared.

Half an hour later, Emmy called everyone to eat. They all came except Sue.

"Where did she go?" Emmy asked.

Holly reported seeing her sister chasing the owl.

"Oh dear," Pam said. "She certainly loves that bird."

Ricky recalled that Sue had run behind the inn. "Maybe she went to the ocean shore. We'd better go after her."

Quickly Emmy covered the food and Pete got Indy's binoculars.

"Fan out," Indy ordered, and they all set off across the dunes, calling the child.

There was no sign of her. When they reached the seashore Pete put the binoculars to his eyes and looked up and down. All that he could see were Jane, Bill, and Gary setting nets on the southern tip of the island. To the north there was nothing but the rocky cliff and then a lonesome stretch of sand, pounded by the incoming tide.

Emmy tried to hide her concern, but Pam noticed her nervousness. "Don't worry, Emmy," she said. "Sue has been taught to stay out of the water unless we are with her."

Now everyone trotted toward the cliff. The sun shone brightly on the white barn, which they could see high above them.

"I hope we can get past those rocks before the

tide cuts us off," said Pete, lengthening his stride. But when they reached the cliff, the waves were crashing against it, sending spray high up among the crags.

"What'll we do now?" Ricky shouted over the roar. "We can't circle the island to hunt for Sue!"

"We might swim around these rocks," Pete suggested.

"No," replied Indy. "The water's too rough, and it would take too much time."

"But going back won't be much faster," Holly put in.

"We could climb the rocks, couldn't we?" asked Pam.

Indy nodded. "Let Pete and me do it. The rest of you stay here."

Pete walked to the side of the cliff away from the spray, then looked up at the forbidding rock formation.

"You go first," Indy said. "I'll follow behind you."

Pete's sneakers found a toe hold in the rocks and he pushed himself upward. Clutching with his fingers and pushing with his feet, the boy made his way up and up. Once he glanced down to see Indy at his heels. "Keep going," the Indian called out. "You're doing fine!"

Halfway up, Pete halted to look for a good handhold among the rocks. He was puffing hard.

"*Keep going!*"

When he found another niche he dug in his fingers and continued up the side of the cliff.

Finally his eyes came level with the top and he could see the white barn not far from him. Standing beside it and looking up with her chubby hands behind her back was Sue.

Quickly Pete climbed over the edge and Indy joined him.

"We found her," the Indian shouted down to the others. "Go back!"

"Sue, what are you doing?" Pete called out. The little girl whirled about and pointed toward the roof of the barn. Beneath the eaves there was a hole in one of the clapboards and sitting in the opening was Fluffy the owl. As they watched, the bird stretched its wings and flew inside. Without a moment's hesitation, Sue dashed around toward the front entrance.

"Stop!" Pete called, racing after her. "We're not allowed near the barn!"

But Sue did not heed him. She wanted her owl.

As Indy ran behind Pete, Mrs. Franklin bolted from the door of her house. She, also, raced toward the barn door. But all of them were too late. Sue, using both hands, pulled the door open and disappeared inside.

Mrs. Franklin's shoulders drooped as Pete came up to her. "Oh, I'm sorry," the boy said. "Sue didn't mean to do any harm, Mrs. Franklin."

Indy also apologized and explained how Sue had been looking for her owl.

72

Just then the little girl stepped out again with Fluffy blinking on her shoulder.

"Oh dear!" Mrs. Franklin said miserably. "Now you know our secret."

She looked down at Sue, whose little cherub face beamed with delight. "Are the white horses your secret?" Sue asked innocently. "They don't look like ghosts to me."

CHAPTER 9

A Dangerous Bird

MRS. FRANKLIN shook her head sadly. "My husband is going to be angry," she said, "when he learns that you've found out our secret."

Sue took the woman's hand in her two little ones. "We won't tell anybody," she promised.

Mrs. Franklin's face softened. "You dear child," she said, and patted Sue's head. Then she smiled at Pete and Indy. "As long as you know, I might as well show you Franz and Josef."

With Fluffy sitting on Sue's shoulder, the little girl followed Mrs. Franklin and Indy into the barn. Pete came last and stood still in amazement when he saw the odd interior.

In the center of the barn was a tanbark circus ring. At the far end were two large stalls, and in each was a beautiful white horse.

The woman walked over to the huge animals and said, "Hello, Franz. We have company, Josef." She patted one of them on the flank as it moved restlessly in the stall.

"Crickets!" said Pete. "They're beauties!"

"I've never seen such fine horses before," Indy declared.

Mrs. Franklin explained that the steeds were

called Lipizzaners. This was an ancient breed, famous in Europe for four centuries.

"Franz and Josef were imported from Vienna," she said, "and we don't want people to know they are here."

"Why not?" asked Sue.

"I'll tell you if you keep the secret," the woman replied.

"Even from Pam and Ricky and Holly and Emmy?" Sue asked.

"Will they promise not to tell?"

"We all will," Pete assured her.

The woman then told them that the horses had been brought from Austria by a groom and now were being trained by her and Mr. Franklin for a circus. "We don't want other circuses to know that we have this act," she said.

"You mean they might copy the horses' tricks?" Pete asked.

Mrs. Franklin smiled. "They couldn't do that. Lipizzaners perform special tricks which are very difficult. They go to school for years to learn them. But spies could copy what my husband and I do. That's why we're keeping it secret."

"See. I told you they weren't ghosts," declared Sue.

"No, of course not," the woman said. She confessed that the last gull team had told her about the phantom horse, but she had never seen it. When Pete told her that he had, she looked puzzled.

"I don't know what that mystery's all about," she declared.

"Then it was your horses we heard the other night," Indy said.

"Yes," Mrs. Franklin replied. "We have to take them out for exercise when it's dark. Several days ago one of them ran away around sunset. I hope nobody saw it."

Indy grinned. "Ricky and Holly did—from the mainland."

"How did the Lipizzaners get on Wicket-ee-nock Island?" Pete asked, as he admired the husky animals. He was told that they were brought over by Captain Wade and Cadwallader Clegg at night.

"Those two men are the only ones who were supposed to know about the horses," Mrs. Franklin said, looking worried, "but I'm afraid there's a spy on the island. Someone has been disturbing Franz and Josef at night. We hear them whinny and stamp, but by the time we get to the barn, the person's gone."

"Maybe it's the bearded man," Pete said.

"Perhaps," she agreed. "Whoever it is makes the animals nervous," she went on unhappily, "so they're hard to handle. I'm afraid our act may not be ready in time."

"How long do you have?" Pete asked.

"We're supposed to join the show in less than a month," she replied.

"I wish we could help you," the boy declared.

"You can," she told him, "by keeping our secret. In return, we may show you how we train the horses. My husband has taken our boat to the mainland for supplies," she continued, "but when he gets back I will see what he says about it."

As they left the barn, Fluffy flapped off Sue's shoulder and flew toward the inn.

"We'd better get back, too," said Indy with a grin. "Our lunch is waiting."

The three said good-by to Mrs. Franklin and hurried down the road. Halfway home they met the other searchers crossing over from the ocean shore.

"Oh, we know a secret. We know a secret!" Sue sang, dancing around them.

"Tell me! Tell me!" Holly begged.

"All right," Pete said, "if you'll all promise never to tell."

"Promise. Scout's honor," Holly said, holding up her right hand.

When the others heard what Sue had discovered, they could hardly believe it.

"Yikes!" Ricky exclaimed. "What a secret!"

"But remember," Pete warned, "you're not to tell anyone."

"Not even Bill and Jane and Gary?" asked Holly.

"Nobody."

"All right. Mum's the word," Emmy declared, and they walked on toward the inn.

"But that still leaves the mystery of the ghost horse," Pam said.

"Maybe he's scaring the Lipizippis at night," Sue spoke up.

"Lipizzaners," Pam said.

"That's an awful big word," Sue remarked with a pout, but repeated it correctly.

When the adventurers reached the inn, Blackie came off the porch to meet them. Emmy quickly reheated the clam broth and served the sandwiches. While they ate, the children talked about the mystery.

"Perhaps there are circus spies on the island," Pam said, "but I don't see why they would need the ghost horse."

"Maybe they want to scare everybody away and then steal Franz and Josef," Ricky suggested.

"No," said Pete. "They couldn't get them off the island without being seen."

"I'll bet the man with the beard is the spy," declared Ricky.

"I've been thinking about his foreign accent," Pete said. "I'll bet he's an Austrian!"

"If he is," Indy said, shaking his head, "that tangles up the mystery all the more."

"Right now I'd like to tangle up some gulls," Ricky said with an impish grin.

"All right," Emmy agreed. "Sue and I'll take a nap."

"Like Fluffy," said the little girl, looking up at the owl on the sign.

"I'll take Blackie and go fishing," Indy put in.

78

"I found an old pole and line behind the inn. Maybe we'll have fresh fish for supper."

"Now remember," Emmy warned the gull catchers, "nothing about the Lipizzaners!"

Pete, Pam, Ricky, and Holly raced toward the gullers' camp. When they reached the tent, Ricky said, "Let's catch some more birds with the fish line." Bill gave the two boys a pole and line. Pam and Holly carried a net trap between them and placed it beside a nest.

Their brothers walked past them and climbed among some high rocks where they found a nest with three large eggs in it. After Pete carefully laid the loop around the edge of it, the two ducked down in a grassy nook and peered out over a boulder at their trap. Overhead the gulls wheeled and cried but none came to sit on the nest. After ten minutes, the boys heard a cry from Holly. "We caught one!"

The brothers got up on their knees to look down at their sisters. Pam was taking a good-sized gull from under the net trap.

"Crickets!" Pete said. "We can't let the girls do better than us."

As he spoke a large black shadow sailed across the sunny rocks. The boys looked up to see a huge gull hovering above them.

"Duck!" exclaimed Pete, and they flattened themselves into the high grass. With wings beating the air, the big bird settled like a dark helicopter onto the nest.

"It's a black-backed gull!" Pete whispered. "We'd better not try to catch it."

"Why not?"

"Pam told me they were dangerous."

Ricky's hands, tightly holding the fish pole itched for action. "But Pete," he said, "the girls caught one."

"Not a black-backed."

As the boys watched, the large gull flapped its wings and stood up. The thought of losing such a prize was more than Ricky could bear. He gave a quick tug on the fish line and snared the bird's legs.

With a hoarse cry the black-backed sea gull soared into the air so strongly that it nearly pulled the pole out of Ricky's hands.

Watching the bird sail off like a kite, the red-head started to reel in the line. The gull pulled until the string was tight. Then suddenly it went slack.

"Look out! He's coming at you!" Pete shouted.

The huge gull dived straight for the back of Ricky's neck. Pete pushed his brother off balance and the bird's beak only nipped at the boy's shirt. The gull flew up and circled for another attack. As it sailed down again Pam and Holly raced toward their brothers.

"Shoo!" shouted Pam, running as fast as she could, but trying not to jounce the captive she held.

80

"Go away!" screamed Holly waving her arms wildly at the bird.

Ricky knelt in the grass and covered his head with his hands as Pete shouted and swiped at the striking gull. With a cry it veered off and swooped up, shaking the loosened noose from its legs.

The redhead looked up, chagrined, as Pete reeled in the line. "Yikes!" Ricky said. "Thanks!"

Then the four children hastened toward the tent where Jane was painting another sea gull. Pete went on down the beach to help Bill and Gary. The other three told Jane what had happened.

"You're lucky you didn't get hurt, Ricky," she said.

After Pam and Holly had colored their bird they put it in the pen to dry. As Holly closed the cage door she glanced toward the water's edge.

"Oh look!" she exclaimed. "There's a gull pecking something red."

"Where?" Pam asked.

Her sister pointed toward a pebbly spot, lapped by the waves. The two girls went to investigate and the younger one picked up a brightly colored sheet of paper. On it was an illustration of a coat of arms. It had been soaked and pecked, but the colors were not faded.

"This must have been dropped here recently," Pam thought.

"What's that? Let me see," Ricky said as he ran up to Holly. He took the soggy picture. It was a

Pete swiped at the striking gull.

red shield with two white horse heads on it and crossed swords beneath them.

Ricky crumpled the paper and was about to fling it into the water when Pam exclaimed, "Wait, Ricky! Don't do that! It might be a clue!"

CHAPTER 10

A Friendly Monster

RICKY handed the soaked paper to Pam, and she spread it out on a rock to dry in the sun. The red-head and Holly ran off to join the gullers, but their sister remained to see that no birds pecked at the red coat of arms.

When the paper dried, Pam put it in her pocket and went to catch gulls with Holly. During the rest of the afternoon she wondered now and then about the coat of arms. Did the horses' heads have anything to do with the Lipizzaners on the island? Was there any connection with the ghost horse?

By now, Pam had become so expert as a guller that she and Holly managed very well by themselves. They ranged the rocky ledges, working as a team.

The sun was getting low in the sky when they heard the station wagon horn in the distance. The girls hastened back to the tent to turn in the net. Ricky and Pete were there, putting their last gull in the drying cage.

"I'm going on," Holly announced. "I'm hungry." She said good-by to the gullers and started down the beach.

Pam waited for her brothers and on the way home she showed Pete the coat of arms. He agreed that it might be a clue. "I wish we could get to a library and find out something about it," he said.

By the time they reached the inn, Emmy had a big pot of baked beans simmering on the fire and fresh fish frying in the pan. Blackie sat patiently by, waiting for his share of Indy's catch.

"Gracious, what a busy day we've had," Emmy remarked, as they enjoyed their evening meal. Sunburned and weary, the Hollisters could barely keep their eyes open. Even Ricky sat still and looked as sleepy as Sam.

"We'd better turn in early tonight," Indy said.

Near dark, Fluffy the owl flew off again and Pam led Sue inside. Now the little girl felt certain that the bird could take care of itself. Pam tucked the dark-haired child into her cot. By the time she was asleep, the others were ready for bed. As Holly got into her cot, Pam, in pajamas, brushed her fluffy golden hair.

"Ho-hum." Pam stifled a yawn. Then she slid between her sheets. But her feet would not go very far!

"Something's wrong!" Pam said as Holly sat up in bed and watched her. Pam again tried to push her feet down between the sheets. Then she exclaimed, "Oh, somebody short-sheeted my bed!" She threw the covers back and found that the white linen had been doubled up, making it impossible for her to stretch out on the cot.

"Holly, did you do this?" Pam asked, cocking her head at the pigtailed girl.

"No, honest."

"Are you sure, you imp!"

Holly held her face in her hands and giggled. "No, I didn't do it. Maybe it was Ricky."

"He wouldn't make it so neat," Pam said. In two steps she pounced on Holly and tickled her until she squealed. Then Pam rearranged her bed and slid all the way down between the cool sheets.

When Pam awoke next morning, she saw her sister quickly dressing. Quietly she half-shut her eyes and watched Holly tiptoe out of the room.

Pam smiled, opened her eyes, hopped from her cot, and dressed. First she made her own bed. Then she short-sheeted Holly's cot.

With a look of satisfaction, Pam strolled to the front of the Lobster Inn, where Indy and Emmy were preparing breakfast for the children.

After they had eaten, the youngsters attended to their chores. By then, enough time had passed for them to go swimming. They pranced along the channel beach, splashing in the cool salty water.

"Look, here come Indy and Emmy!" Ricky called out delightedly. The grownups dived into the water and swam about with long graceful strokes. As Indy passed close by, Ricky splashed him. Indy splashed back, and before long, a water fight was in full swing.

Sue opened her mouth to say something, but got a faceful of water. She choked and sputtered, pointing out across the water. The splashing stopped and they all looked. Rowing rapidly toward them was Sleepy Sam.

As Pam slapped Sue on the back to make her stop coughing, Pete hailed the clam digger.

"Hi, Sleepy!" Pete called out. "Are you going to dig for some more clams?"

The droopy-eyed man shipped his oars and drifted alongside the swimmers. "I've got news," he said.

"Another telegram?" asked Pam.

Sleepy Sam shook his head. "The salvage boat is going to raise the ferry today."

"That'll be great!" Ricky exclaimed. "Can we row out and watch it?"

"Sure. But I only have room for four of you."

The youngsters pulled the clam digger's skiff onto the beach and plied him with questions. A special salvage craft was due to arrive in the channel at two o'clock, towing a barge with a large derrick. It was decided that Sue should remain on shore with Indy and Emmy.

A diver, Sleepy Sam told them, would go down and attach cables to the sunken vessel. Then the derrick would lift the ferry right onto the deck of the barge.

The Hollisters could hardly wait for the time to come. In order to make the hours pass more quickly, the three younger children helped Sleepy Sam dig buckets of clams. The older two hastened to join the gullers.

When they returned for luncheon, Pete and Pam found a pot of chowder bubbling over the outdoor

"I've got news," said Sleepy Sam.

fire. Sleepy Sam sat on the porch steps with Sue beside him.

"We helped to catch our own lunch," said the little girl proudly.

As Emmy ladled cups of steaming chowder for the hungry adventurers, Indy came around the corner of the inn. "I tied Blackie in back," he said to Sam, "so you can eat in peace."

When they had finished, Pete, Pam, Ricky, and Holly changed to clean shorts and tops, then ran down to the rowboat.

"Come on, let's go out and wait for the salvage barge," Pete suggested. With Sam's permission, the Hollisters pushed the boat into the water and the clam digger rowed slowly to the middle of the channel. As he circled around the mast of the sunken ferryboat, they heard a whistle in the distance. Scanning the sparkling water, they saw a large boat approaching, towing a barge.

Sleepy Sam backed off a distance, and the Hollisters waved and cheered as both vessels anchored alongside the sunken hull.

Among them Pete spotted Captain Wade.

"He thinks a heap of the *Mermaid*," Sleepy Sam said, "and wants to be right on the spot when they raise her."

"Yikes! That derrick could lift a whale!" Ricky remarked as he gazed up at the towering superstructure on the barge.

"Look, the diver's getting ready," Pam said. On the deck, a man slipped into a diving suit. A brown globe-shaped helmet was placed over his head and fastened securely around his neck.

While two men controlled the hose line sticking out of the helmet, the diver went over the side and disappeared in a swirling circle of bubbles. Then the derrick lowered a long cable into the water. Time passed as the salvage crew busied themselves on the barge.

Suddenly Ricky exclaimed, "Look! Those bubbles are coming close to our boat."

Pete peered over the side and saw the diver's brass helmet dimly in the water below. It rose and *swoosh*—broke out of the water. Through the glass faceplate the grinning diver winked, then he submerged as fast as he had come up.

The Hollisters giggled and Holly said, "He looked like some funny sea monster!"

As she spoke the bubbles trailed off toward the barge. Several minutes later the diver was hauled aboard and his helmet removed.

As Sleepy Sam rowed closer, the diver grinned and shouted, "Sorry if I scared you. I just wanted to say 'Hello'!"

Laughing, the children called "Hello," and waved.

"Stand back now," bellowed a man on the barge. "We're going to lift the ferry."

Sleepy Sam shared the oars with Pete and they rowed rapidly away. When they had reached a safe distance, a great grinding and chugging noise sounded on the barge. The derrick cable drew taut. At the same time, the mast of the ferry began to rise higher above the water. Up and up came the sunken boat. Now the children could see that it was cradled snugly in a cable sling. Finally the entire ferryboat was lifted into the air and swung onto the wide deck of the barge.

"Hurray!" Pete cried out, Ricky whistled shrilly and the girls clapped.

As the two vessels started slowly toward the shore, the clam digger rowed alongside the barge and the Hollisters talked with the crewmen. They learned that the ferry would be kept on the barge while repairs were being made. Then it would be set down in the ferry slip once more.

Now they were close enough to Cliffport to recognize people standing on the dock. Among them was the Snowman. He waved at the children.

"Let's go ashore and get ice cream," said Ricky.

Pete agreed. "And we could check on that telegram, if you wouldn't mind waiting for us," he added to the clam digger.

"You go ahead," said their boatman, and told them where to find the telegraph office. Pam offered to get him a snow-stick, but he said he did not like ice cream.

As the children climbed up on the pier, the Snowman trundled his cart over to them. He reached into it and said, "Four snow-sticks coming right up!"

As Pete paid, the Snowman said, "I guess you

must be happy now that the ferryboat is raised. That means you can go home."

Holly stopped with the snow-stick halfway to her mouth. "Oh no!" she exclaimed. "I forgot all about that!"

"We don't want to leave," Ricky said. "We're having a great time."

"I heard there were funny goings on over there," the man said in a low voice. "Maybe it isn't safe."

"You mean the ghost horse?" asked Ricky. "We're not afraid of that. In fact, we think it's just a—" He stopped as Pete gave him a warning nudge.

"Come on," Pete said quickly. "We've got to go." The children said good-by to the Snowman and moved off.

"Yikes," Ricky grumbled. "I wasn't doing anything wrong."

"A detective shouldn't talk so much," the older boy said sternly.

Ricky looked crestfallen as they left the dock, but by the time they had walked a block to the telegraph office he was cheerful again.

As they entered, they saw a thin young clerk behind the counter. Pete identified himself and asked how the telegram had been received in the office.

"A man called up from a coin box," he said, "right here in Cliffport."

As the children left the telegraph office they met the Snowman outside the door.

"So you sent a telegram," he said. "I'll bet it was to your mother and daddy to say you were coming home."

"No—" Ricky began, but feeling Pete's eyes on him, he said no more.

The Snowman's round face was full of amazement. "You didn't wire anybody?" He chuckled. "I thought sure I'd guessed it right."

"Well, we have to go now," said Pete. "So long!"

The children said good-by and hastened away.

"He has good ice cream," Holly remarked, "but he's awful nosy."

At the dock they found Sleepy Sam patiently waiting in his boat. Pete helped him row back to Wicket-ee-nock.

When the bow of the skiff touched the sand, the four Hollisters jumped out and thanked the clam digger. Then they raced up to the Lobster Inn to tell their news.

"That was an exciting afternoon!" Emmy exclaimed, then added, "I have a message for you."

She told them that Mr. Franklin had visited the inn that afternoon. "He invited all of us to his barn after supper tonight," she said.

When the meal was over, Pam tied the dog on the porch.

"We're leaving you here, Blackie," she said. "You might make the horses nervous." She gave him a pat and ran to join the others who had started up the beach.

"I am glad the Franklins like us," Holly said as they walked toward the big white barn. When they reached it, the door was ajar several inches. Indy pushed it open and they stepped in. The sight that greeted them was something they had never seen before!

CHAPTER 11

A Sudden Squall

Two Lipizzan horses were standing on their hind legs in the center of the ring. Riding them were Mr. and Mrs. Franklin. But how different the couple looked!

This time the horse trainers were not dressed in dungarees. The woman, sitting sidesaddle, wore a lovely blue velvet gown with a lace collar. Her hair was piled high in curls and she wore a perky blue hat with a huge white plume. Her husband had on white riding breeches and a scarlet coat. His boots were polished and his black cockade hat was trimmed with gold braid.

As the Hollisters gasped in surprise, the Lipizzaners came down on all fours, then immediately broke into a slow and stately trot. Pam started to clap and the others joined in.

The horses approached, knelt on one knee, and the Franklins dismounted.

"You didn't tell us you were circus performers!" Pete said.

The woman smiled and patted Sue's head. "You never asked us," she replied sweetly.

"Yikes, you look different!" Ricky exclaimed.

Pam gave her brother a stern look for his undiplomatic remark. Ricky hastened to add, "Well, you know what I mean. You're all dressed up now."

"Of course," Mrs. Franklin said, adding that they put on this dress rehearsal just for the Hollisters.

Mr. Franklin, looking handsome in his uniform, told them about the beautiful horses. He explained that a Lipizzaner is born pitch-black or brown. The coat gradually grows lighter, sometimes not reaching the typical snow-white until the horse is seven years old.

"Then I'd be a white Lippizzaner by now!" Rick said proudly.

"You jump around like a horse sometimes," Holly remarked.

"Now let us show you some of the things which Franz and Josef have learned," Mrs. Franklin said. "You saw them do the pesade, that is, balancing on their hind legs."

As the children looked on spellbound, the Franklins made the horses do other tricks. First was the Spanish walk, a spirited trot with high knee action. Next the horses raised their front legs off the ground and balanced on their haunches as the Hollisters, Indy, and Emmy cheered.

"That was the levade," Mr. Franklin announced. "The last and most difficult feat is the capriole." This was a wonderful leap in which the horses, remaining horizontal to the ground, sprang five feet high. They landed on all four legs in the same place from which they had sprung up.

"I think you're more than ready for the circus," Indy said when the Franklins had finished their act.

"I hope so," the man replied. "But the horses are still very nervous. Something is bothering them."

"Indeed," his wife went on, "I hope it doesn't spoil our act."

"It's probably that snooper around here," Ricky said, wrinkling his nose, but he added bravely, "We'll be around to protect your horses."

After thanking the Franklins for the wonderful show they had put on, the visitors trooped out of the barn. Pete, in the lead, looked toward the sea and let out a small cry. He saw the top of a man's head disappear behind a crag at the edge of the cliff. Pete ran over, but the spy was out of reach, climbing down over the rocks. The fellow glanced up and his eyes met the boy's gaze for a moment.

It was the stranger with the beard!

Quickly Pete started down after him. In his haste, he slipped and slid several feet before he caught himself on a tiny rock ledge.

"Help!" Pete cried out. He tried to brace himself with his feet, but found only a small toe hold.

He looked up to see Indy's face above him.

"Hold on!" Indy shouted and dashed off. After what seemed like a year, he returned with a rope. He had already fashioned a noose, which he dropped down over Pete's shoulders.

97

Suddenly there was a mighty tug and the boy was lifted up inch by inch.

When Pete, scraped and bruised, finally reached the top of the cliff, he saw that the Lipizzaner named Franz was pulling the other end of the rope.

"Oh my! What a scare you gave us," Mrs. Franklin said.

"I—I was scared, too," Pete said, but assured the frightened onlookers that no bones had been broken.

"That bearded man," Emmy explained, "has caused more trouble!"

Pete looked over the cliff edge. There was no sign of the fellow. "I'll get him," Pete thought. "Maybe he lives in those caves in the rocks."

The boy was quiet all the way home. At bedtime Indy asked him what was the matter and he said, "May I go to the mainland and rent a boat, Indy?"

"I suppose so. Why?"

"I'd like to go around the island to see if I can spot where the prowler lives."

"All right, but be careful. Maybe I should go with you."

"I'll be okay," said the boy.

"Well, take Pam along," Indy advised.

Just then a screech came from the girl's bedroom and Holly called out, "Who short-sheeted my cot?" The pigtailed girl rushed in wearing pajamas. She put her hands on her hips and said, "Ricky, you did it, I bet!"

"Me?" asked Ricky, looking innocent.

"Yes, you. And you short-sheeted Pam! You're not fooling me," she added, and hurried back to remake her bed. "Just wait till tomorrow," she thought.

By midmorning the youngsters were swimming again. Holly left the water first, and went directly into the inn. A few minutes later she emerged from the boys' bedroom with a grin on her face. "That'll fix him," she said to herself.

After lunch she and Ricky raced off to help the gullers. Pete told Pam his plan to rent a boat.

"How'll we get to Cliffport and back again?" she asked.

Pete reported that he had seen Sleepy Sam digging clams on the beach. "Maybe he'll take us."

When they told Indy, he gave them enough money to rent a motorboat.

Then Pete and Pam ran up the beach and found Sleepy Sam loading buckets of clams into his skiff. He said he would be glad to have their company.

When he let them off on the Cliffport dock, the first person they saw was the Snowman. "Well, back again!" he exclaimed, and reached into his ice chest. "Here, have a treat on me."

"You shouldn't give away your ice cream," Pam said.

"You're special favorites," replied the Snowman.

But Pam paid him for the two snow-sticks, anyway.

"How's that mystery coming on?" the vendor asked as the youngsters bit into the ice cream.

"It's quiet," Pete said.

"We'd like to rent a boat," Pam interrupted, trying to change the subject.

"There's the place you want," the Snowman said. He pointed to the boat livery beside the pier.

"Thanks," Pete said, and the children walked off the dock. The boat livery was a little frame structure built over the water and surrounded by a catwalk. Small craft of all kinds were moored there, rocked by the lapping water. Pete saw that the outboard motors were tilted up and protected with plastic covers. Each boat had a number painted on the bow. The children walked down several steps onto the catwalk, then opened the door marked "Office." A young man with blond hair sat in a chair, his feet up on the desk.

"We'd like to rent a boat," Pete said.

"The owner's out, but I can take care of you," the fellow said, rising to his feet. Pete and Pam stared in surprise.

"You're the man who was in a boat stuck on a sand bar off Wicket-ee-nock," Pete said, "and you cooked the sea-gull eggs."

The man's blue eyes slid over the children coolly. "Says who?" he replied, pushed past them, and walked out.

"What's your name?" asked Pete, following him.

"You're pretty nosy," the fellow said. "My name's Scally. What kind of a boat do you want?"

Pete said a medium-sized one with a good outboard motor.

"Take number twelve," the man advised, and the boy paid for two days' rent in advance.

Pete stepped into the craft, uncovered the motor, and found that it was the same make as their own on Pine Lake in Shoreham.

"Do you know how to run it?" Scally asked.

"Yes," Pete said. "May we have an extra can of gas?"

"Wait a minute." The man walked back into the office and returned with a full tin which he handed to Pete.

"Thanks," the boy said. After Pam untied the mooring ropes, Pete shoved off, started the motor, and set out across the channel toward Wicket-ee-nock.

"Crickets! This is keen!" Pete said as the motor purred, sending the little craft straight as an arrow.

When they neared the shore of the island, Pete turned south, steering a course about thirty yards offshore. As they rounded the southern tip, the gullers, Ricky, and Holly waved to them. On the ocean side of the island, the water was rougher, and the boat bobbed up and down in the swells.

When they ran past the rocks at the foot of the cliff, both children looked hard for a sign of someone living in the caverns. But they saw only the dark cave mouths with the water pounding on the rocks below them.

"We're too far away to see well," Pete said. "I'm going to run closer to the cliff."

He turned the boat about and headed south again. This time they went more slowly but still could not look into the caves. They peered carefully among the huge rocks, but caught no glimpse of a tent or lean-to.

The youngsters were so intent on scouting the shore that they did not notice the sky suddenly grow dark. It was not until Pete had turned north again, to come even closer to the cliff, that he felt several drops of rain pelt his cheek.

"Look!" Pam cried, pointing seaward. "There's a squall coming."

As she spoke, the outboard motor sputtered and stopped. "Crickets! We can't be out of gas already," Pete said. He quickly unscrewed the cap and looked into the tank. Empty! Pete reached for the spare can of fuel and poured it into the tank. He tried to start the motor. It would not even kick over.

Pete lifted the gas can and held the spout to his nose. The familiar smell of fuel was not there!

"Pam!" Pete cried as the boat began to pitch on the roughened sea. "There's only water in this can!"

"That mean Scally!" his sister exclaimed.

"Look! There's a squall coming!"

Suddenly rain whipped across the boat in sheets. "What'll we do now?" Pam called out as the water streaked down her hair.

"Guide it to shore as best I can," the boy said. He half stood in the boat with his hand on the tiller, looking for a safe place between the jagged rocks.

The little craft pitched more violently as it neared shore. It seemed to Pete that there were only rocks, rocks, rocks!

Suddenly, as if out of nowhere, a man appeared among the boulders below the caves. He wore a raincoat with the collar raised and yellow sou'wester hat with the brim turned down. He motioned for Pete to keep to the right.

"Who is he?" Pam called out above the roar of the waves.

"I can't see his face, either," Pete shouted. "It's raining too hard."

"Maybe we'd better do what he says," Pam said. The same thought was going through the minds of both children. Was the stranger trying to save them, or make them crash upon the rocks?

"We'll have to paddle by hand, Pam!" The brother and sister knelt in the left side of the boat, paddling as best they could with both hands. Now the craft was veering off, as the stranger directed. Then a huge wave picked the boat up and hurled it directly at the rocky shore.

CHAPTER 12

Three Strikes

RIDING high on the breaker, the boat missed two jagged rocks and slid to a hissing halt on a sandy open spot.

Pete and Pam jumped out, pulled the craft under an overhanging ledge, and huddled against the base of the cliff. The huge waves pounded and churned. Sometimes they reached waist high, and the children could hardly keep the boat from drifting out into the boiling sea.

But gradually the squall slackened. A white rift showed in the dark clouds. The wind ceased to blow. The waves died down and in ten minutes were lapping at the feet of the youngsters. Both were drenched and shivering.

"Crickets!" Pete said. "That was a close one!"

"That man saved us," Pam remarked, "by showing us the right direction to land."

Pete shuddered at the thought of what might have happened. "The rocks would have crushed our boat like an eggshell," he said, and added, "Do you suppose that was the mysterious foreigner again?"

"I don't know," Pam said.

They scanned the rocks but saw no sign of the stranger.

"Look!" She pointed to a yellow object tucked

into a crevice in the rocks. Pete pulled it out. "It's that man's rain hat."

The Hollisters realized that the sou'wester must have been pressed into the nook on purpose.

"And here's the reason why," Pete said. Inside the hat was a wet note written in pencil. It said, "Hollisters—you are in danger. Go home."

Pete whistled. "First the man saves us, then he warns us. I wonder who he can be?"

"Well, he can't be too bad," Pam reasoned. Then she shook her head and added, "But where does he hide? And why?"

Now the waves had subsided enough to leave a narrow strip of sand between the rocks and the water's edge.

Pulling their boat along, Pete and Pam passed the cliff and placed the powerless craft high on the beach, where the tides could not reach it.

They started back on foot, taking the yellow hat with them. They had not gone far before they saw Indy, Emmy, and the other children running along the shore to meet them. Ricky and Holly had reported seeing their brother and sister round the point in the motorboat.

"And when the storm came up we were terribly worried about you," Emmy said, giving Pam a hug.

As Pete told what had happened, Indy became more and more indignant. "What a mean trick!" he exclaimed. "Giving you water instead of gasoline."

"It could have been very serious," Emmy said. "Thank goodness you're all safe."

The grownups were mystified when they heard about the stranger who had left the note in his hat.

"Yikes," Holly said. "He knows all about us. What'll we do with the boat?" was the next question.

It was decided to leave the rented craft until next morning. "We can siphon some gasoline from the station wagon," Indy said, "and start the motor again. I'll have a few things to say to Scally when I see him!"

That night Holly, surprising everyone, went to bed first. When Pam prepared to retire, her sister had a little smile on her face, which looked angelic in the candlelight. Holly was not asleep. She was listening quietly for Ricky's voice in the next room.

There, Ricky hopped into his pajamas quickly and shoved his feet between the sheets. A surprised look came over his freckled face but he did not make any outcry.

Pete glanced over from his bed and grinned. "Short-sheeted?" he asked. Then at the expression on Ricky's face, Pete broke into laughter.

Ricky said nothing. Instead, his eyes narrowed as a scheme crossed his mind. He had been short-sheeted and planned to do something about it, but not now. Ricky fixed the covers and was fast asleep even before Holly.

Next morning Pete noticed that Ricky was

dawdling about the bedroom. When the older boy started to make up his cot, Ricky said, "Oh, don't bother. Let me do it today."

"Okay, if you want to." When Pete hastened out, Ricky short-sheeted his brother's bed, muttering, "Thinks he can fool me, does he!"

While the girls helped to clean the breakfast utensils, Ricky and Pete walked to the station wagon with Indy.

"How are you going to siphon the gasoline?" asked Pete.

Ricky said, "We need a small hose, don't we, Indy?"

Before the man could reply, Pete snapped his fingers. "I know where we can find one!" Much to the surprise of Indy, Pete lifted the hood of the car and pointed to a small tube leading from a water jar to the windshield wipers.

"We can use this and put it back again," Pete said.

"Good thinking," Indy remarked, and Ricky secretly admired his brother's ingenuity.

In a few minutes Indy had siphoned off enough gas for the outboard motor. Then Pete replaced the tube and closed the hood of the car.

"We'll be back soon!" Indy called out as they trudged off behind the old inn. He and the two boys hastened to the oceanside with the can of gasoline, but when they reached the spot where the boat had been left, all three gazed about in amazement. It was gone!

"Who could have taken it?" Indy exclaimed.

"Someone with gasoline," said Pete.

"This mystery is getting me!" Indy declared, much annoyed.

"Now we owe for a boat," Ricky remarked.

"We'll see about that," said Indy. "Scally has some explaining to do first."

By the time they returned and told the others the disappointing news, Sleepy Sam had arrived and was digging for clams in his favorite spot not far from the inn.

"Just the man we're looking for!" Indy said as the travelers walked over to him. "We'd like you to take some of us to the mainland, Sleepy Sam."

"Sure, sure."

"But first we'll help you dig," Indy said.

Clams seemed to pop out of the sand as the Hollisters dug happily. When two buckets were filled, Pete, Pam, and Holly stepped into Sleepy Sam's boat with Indy. Ricky, Emmy, and Sue remained behind to go see the gullers.

"I'll tell them about Scally and the trick he played on you," Ricky promised.

As Sleepy Sam shoved off, Emmy cried, "Oh, wait!" She took a slip of paper from her pocket and handed it to Indy. "Here's a list of groceries we need," she said. "And don't forget the bacon," she called as the boat headed for Cliffport.

At first Indy joined Sleepy Sam at the oars. Halfway over they were spelled by Pete and Pam.

When they arrived at the pier, Indy said, "We'll be ready to go back with you in about an hour."

"All right," the boatman replied. "I'll sell my clams and meet you here."

Indy and the three children marched off like an army to the boat livery office. But the place was closed, and Scally nowhere to be seen.

"This ought to be reported to Cadwallader Clegg!" Indy declared, and they set off up the long hill. They arrived tired, hot, and thirsty. Again, disappointment. There was a sign on Cadwallader's door. It read: "Gone fishing. Back tomorrow."

"Phew!" Pete exclaimed. "What a day."

"I could use a nice, cold snow-stick!" Holly said as they started down toward the town.

"We didn't see our friend, the Snowman," Pam remarked as they neared the foot of the hill.

"Maybe it's too early for him to be out," Pete said.

As the youngsters trooped down the main street, Pam touched Indy's arm and said, "Holly and I have an errand to do at the library. We'll meet you at the dock."

"All right," was the reply. "Pete and I'll pick up the supplies now."

The boy asked his sisters if they were going to get some books.

"No, it's about a clue," Pam replied. She and Holly took hands and crossed the street toward a small one-room building bearing the sign "FREE PUBLIC LIBRARY."

The inside smelled like polished woodwork and new books. Pam sniffed as she entered and whispered to Holly, "I like libraries."

Her remark was overheard by a young woman behind a desk. "I'm glad you like libraries," she said. "Is there something I can do for you?"

"Thank you," Pam replied. "We're looking for a book about coats of arms—you know, the kind that knights and kings had in the olden days."

The librarian smiled. "That's called 'heraldry,'" she said.

Pam reached in her pocket and pulled out the picture she had found on Wicket-ee-nock.

"Yes, indeed. That's a coat of arms," the librarian said, "but I'm sorry that we don't have a book on it."

Pam looked downcast, but the young woman continued brightly, "Oh, don't feel sad. If you're going to be around town for a few days, I can get a book for you."

"Where?" asked Holly.

"From the library in Boston," came the reply. "I'll telephone there immediately for a book on heraldry. They'll send it to me."

Pam and Holly thanked the librarian, then hastened off to meet Pete and Indy. On the way they looked for the Snowman but did not see him.

At the dock they found their brother and Indy

putting a big bag of groceries in Sleepy Sam's boat. The clam digger had not returned yet.

"Any luck?" Indy asked the girls.

"No, not today," Pam replied.

"That makes three strikes on us, so I guess we're out," Pete said glumly.

"How about a nice cool bottle of soda pop?" Indy suggested. They found a place close by and Indy said, "My, but it's good to wet your whistle." This made Holly giggle, so that some of the bubbles went up her nose.

When they had finished, Indy said, "Well, we couldn't do anything we wanted to, so let's go back to Wicket-ee-nock." Sleepy Sam had sold his clams and was ready to row them across the channel.

The hungry travelers arrived in time for lunch, and the rest of the day was spent swimming and helping the gullers.

Shortly before bedtime, Mrs. Franklin appeared and invited the children to come to their barn next day. She stayed long enough for a cup of tea with Indy and Emmy, then started for home along the moonlit beach.

As the children were going to bed, Pete let out a shout. "Who short-sheeted my cot!" he cried. "Did you do it, Ricky?"

The redhead only shrugged and his brother said, "I know, it was Pam!"

"Oh, it was not," came his sister's voice from next door. In the candlelight Pete crept into the

"What's going on here?"

girls' room and plopped a pillow on Pam's head. Instantly, Holly sprang to her sister's defense and whacked Pete with her pillow. Hearing the noise, Ricky joined the fracas.

"What's going on here?" asked Emmy as she hastened into the room amid the flying pillows.

"Pam short-sheeted me!" Pete said.

"I didn't, but someone played the trick on me," said Pam.

"Me too," Ricky cried.

"And me, too," said Holly.

"We'll have to get to the bottom of this," declared Indy, arriving on the scene in his pajamas. "Who started this whole short-sheeting business?"

Each of the older children said No and Sue piped up, "I didn't sheet-short either."

"Well, Blackie didn't start it, that's for sure," Indy said.

Suddenly Pam's eyes sparkled as she noticed a half-smile across Emmy's face. "Oh," she said, putting her hand to her mouth. "Emmy, are you the rascal who started the whole thing?"

A girlish smile brightened Emmy's face. "I must confess," she said, and the five Hollister children screeched at the same time.

CHAPTER 13

An Odd Brand

SUE jumped up on her cot, flung her arms around Emmy, and said gleefully, "You are a scamp like Mommy says I am."

All the youngsters were delighted that Emmy Roades had played such a funny trick.

"That will teach you," she said, laughing, "not to go blaming people until you have proof."

When the travelers arrived at the Franklins' barn next day, they found the horse trainers dressed in their dungarees.

"Good morning," Mr. Franklin said, dismounting and walking over to them. "I don't know what to do with Franz and Josef. They're as nervous as kittens!"

"Did someone bother them during the night?" Pete asked.

"That must have been it," the trainer replied. Then he added that he had planned to give the children rides that morning.

"I see you're dressed for it," Mrs. Franklin said as she, too, dismounted. All the Hollisters were wearing dungarees. "Have you ever been on horseback before?"

"Oh yes," Pam assured her. "We're not afraid."

The woman looked at their eager faces and smiled. "I can see that," she said. While she and her husband unsaddled the white horses, the animals snorted and shied.

"Steady, Franz," Mrs. Franklin said. She patted the big horse and spoke softly into his twitching ear.

"Kindness is very important in training these animals," Mr. Franklin told the visitors quietly. "They must be treated firmly but always gently, and never overworked."

When the Lipizzaners were standing still again, Mr. Franklin lifted Sue and Pam aboard Franz, while Indy hoisted Pete and Ricky onto Josef.

At a command from Mrs. Franklin, the horses pranced about the ring, their heads held high.

"Yikes! I'm in a circus!" Ricky cried out happily. After several times around, the Franklins halted the Lipizzaners. The youngsters slid to the ground, and Holly was boosted onto Josef.

Around the ring she went, bouncing on the broad back of the circus horse. But suddenly, without warning, Josef reared back. Holly tumbled to the ground, amid the shouts of the onlookers.

As the Franklins ran toward the horse, it backed up several paces and stood still directly over Holly. The trainers seized the bridle and the pigtailed girl scrambled out from under the animal.

"Holly, are you all right?" Emmy cried as she ran up to her.

Holly bobbed her head. "Sure, I'm fine. But I saw something funny, Emmy." Then in the same breath she added, "Do they brand circus horses?"

"What do you mean?" asked Mrs. Franklin.

"I saw a brand on the underneath side of Josef," Holly replied.

The trainers exchanged glances, and the man said, "A brand? Where?"

Holly bent down and pointed between the horse's forelegs. The Franklins looked, too.

"She's right," the woman said. "You didn't tell me about that, Amos."

"I've never noticed it before," the man replied as he peered at the brand more closely. Then the visitors examined the odd marking. It looked like a crescent moon with a tiny star between the two tips.

"It's something like a Turkish insignia," Pam said.

"Maybe there's a brand on Franz, too," Ricky suggested. He peered beneath the second horse, standing nearby. "Yes, there is one," he called out, "but it's different."

The horse acted skittish, and Mr. Franklin calmed him, then studied the marking.

This one looked like a triangle with a small ball on top of it.

"Another mystery," Mrs. Franklin said with a sigh. "Amos," she directed, "go get the record book, please."

Her husband went to the house and returned with a black book. In it were written the histories of Franz and Josef from the day they were born in the mountains of eastern Europe.

The Franklins turned page after page, reading carefully. When they had finished the woman said, "There is not a thing about brands on these horses."

"Then the marks must have been put on in America," Pam said.

"But by whom?" Emmy asked.

Mr. Franklin suggested that Max Stein might have done it. He was the groom who brought the horses from Vienna to the United States.

"Mr. Stein stayed here with us for several days, then left suddenly," Mrs. Franklin told them. Nothing had been heard from him since.

"The brands won't do Franz and Josef any harm," she went on, "but I'm worried about how nervous they are growing. Poor Holly," she added, "I'm so glad you weren't hurt."

"I'd like to catch the prowler who's disturbing our horses," Mr. Franklin declared. "I've kept watch outside the barn at night, but I've never seen him yet."

"Let us help you," Pete said. "Ricky and I could sleep in the barn and give the alarm if someone comes in."

"And I could post myself outside the door in a sleeping bag," Indy added.

The Franklins thought this was a good idea and consented to let the Shoreham detectives try their plan that evening.

Then the sleuths said good-by and left their

friends to continue training the beautiful white circus horses.

That afternoon, while the boys helped Indy repair some loose shutters on the inn, Holly and Pam went off to help the gullers.

"We've already caught plenty for the day," Jane said, and added, "How would you like to watch the birds nesting from a distance? You can use binoculars."

"That would be fun," Pam replied.

"Here, then," Jane said, handing her a pair of field glasses. "These are very powerful." She pointed toward a grassy dune. "There's a nice high spot over there. Why don't you and Holly make that your lookout?"

The girls climbed to the top, sat cross-legged in the grass, and began to watch the gull nests. First Holly scanned the nesting rocks, then turned the binoculars over to Pam.

When the sisters tired of watching the birds, they swept the glasses over the ocean and island. Pam was studying the dunes near the channel, when suddenly she let out a cry. "I think I've found it!"

"What?"

"Where that mystery man lives!" She handed the binoculars to Holly. "Look," she said, "at the bottom of that dune over there."

"Yikes," Holly exclaimed. "I think you're right." What she saw was part of a flat wooden roof nearly hidden by sand.

"Come on, let's investigate," Pam said.

The girls hurried across two sand hills, and on top of the third Pam clutched Holly's arm.

"There it is!"

They dropped flat and peered at the base of the next dune. Sticking out of it was the front of a small tumbledown shack. The rest had been buried by the sand. The door was gone, but the opening was in shadow.

"Do you think the man is in there?" Holly whispered.

"Follow me," Pam said quietly. "We'll see."

She slid back down the dune and went around it. Hearts pounding, the sisters approached the shack from the side. Several steps from the doorway, Pam stopped. She and Holly stood listening. Except for the wash of the waves on the beach there was no sound.

Pam picked up a handful of sand and tossed it in front of the entrance. The girls waited. In the distance a gull cried, but there was no noise from the shack.

Holly threw more sand. Still no sign of life!

Cautiously they walked up to the doorway and peered into the dim interior. No one was there. As they stepped in, their footsteps grated on the sandy floor. Sand trickled down on them from cracks between the roof boards.

"Look," Pam said softly, and pointed to the telltale yellow raincoat in the back. "The man who lives here is the one who saved Pete and me."

"Do you think the man is in there?" Holly whispered.

"Do you think he's the bearded man?" asked Holly.

"Who knows?" Pam shrugged.

The girls also noted a sleeping bag and a wooden crate with five cans of food on it in a neat row.

"I feel sorry for anybody who has to live here," she added.

"I do, too," Holly agreed. "It's gloomy and you get sand down your neck."

Quickly they scrambled out again. The girls ran as fast as they could back to Jane. She was coloring a sea gull and stopped to ask the flushed children why they had been running so hard. Pam told her, handed back the binoculars, and said, "We're going to get Pete and Ricky right away. We'll all stand watch until that man comes back."

Jane called to Bill and Gary, who were setting gull traps nearby. The boys were impressed to hear what the sisters had discovered.

"That must be an old fisherman's shack," Gary said, and explained that it was buried because the dunes shifted with the winds.

"If you need any help catching the fellow, you can call on us," Bill added.

When they reached the Lobster Inn, the breathless girls reported their discovery.

"Now we're getting somewhere with the mystery!" Pete said exultantly.

"Yikes! Come on, we'll have a stake-out, men!" Ricky declared.

Indy advised the children to stay well concealed. If the stranger returned to his makeshift dwelling, Ricky was to race back and tell Indy.

"Then I'll nab him myself," the Indian said, "and get to the bottom of all this."

Before long the excited detectives were settled behind dunes and clumps of high grass. But the afternoon wore on slowly. The children watched the shack in vain. Nobody came.

"Maybe the fellow was scared away for good," said Holly, peeking through the coarse grass at Pam.

"But we can't give up hope," Pam replied. However, the two boys seemed ready to give up, at least for the moment, as suppertime neared.

"The man probably has seen us," Pete said. "That's why he won't come back."

After supper, Indy and Pete concealed themselves behind a dune and watched the shelter, but by nightfall nobody had returned to it.

"Come on, Indy," Pete said. "We'd better get over to the Lipizzaners' barn before it gets too late."

They returned to the inn, picked up Ricky, took several flashlights, and walked briskly to the Franklins' place. The horse trainer swung off the porch when he saw them coming and led them into the barn.

There Pete and Ricky made themselves comfortable in piles of straw at one side of the stalls.

Indy said good night to them and slipped into the sleeping bag outside the barn door.

"Give a whistle if you want me," said Mr. Franklin, and strode back to the house.

Inside the barn the only noises were an occasional thump or snort from the restless horses. The brothers finally fell asleep in the sweet-smelling hay.

Suddenly Pete was wide awake! He glanced at the stalls and saw a light shining on the underside of Franz. Pete reached over and touched his brother. Ricky was there—not in the stall. The redhead sat up with a start.

"Who's there?" Pete called out bravely.

The light flicked out, leaving him in darkness. Pete felt for his flashlight but could not find it immediately. Then he heard the intruder run across the barn floor. Then the door banged.

"Indy, catch him!" Pete shouted. He and Ricky ran to the door, nearly bumping into Indy, who was entering.

"Did you catch him?" Pete asked, flashing his light about.

"Catch who?"

"The prowler in the barn," Pete replied. "He ran out the door, didn't he?"

"Nobody came this way," Indy said.

CHAPTER 14

An Ancient Clue

"Yikes!" said Ricky. "Somebody ran out. We heard the door."

"I did, too," said Indy, "but no one came past me."

"Then there must be some other way out of this place," Pete declared, flashing his light about the barn.

"Let's go tell the Franklins," said Ricky, and headed for the door. But Pete caught him by the arm.

"There's no use doing that now," his brother said. Pete reasoned that the Franklins were upset enough, and Indy agreed with him.

The first thing they did was to calm the nervous horses. "Easy, Franz. Quiet there, Josef," Indy said, stroking the circus steeds.

At the same time, Pete told what he had seen and added, "I think it's obvious now, Indy. The prowler is either looking for those brand marks or is studying them."

"I agree," said Indy as he turned away from the horses. "Now let's search for the secret exit." The trio looked into every nook and cranny of the barn, but could not see where anybody could escape.

125

Ricky's spine tingled. "Yikes," he said, "maybe he's still in the barn!"

Indy had to admit that this was a possibility. "I'll sleep inside here with you, Ricky," he said, "and Pete can guard the door."

The watchers slept lightly during the rest of the night. They awakened at daylight, left the Lipizzaners, and arrived at the Lobster Inn to find Fluffy already asleep on the sign. None of the travelers were awake, either.

"Come on, get up, lazy bones," Ricky shouted as he stomped through the old inn.

"Did anything happen?" Pam asked sleepily.

"Plenty!" Pete said. "We'll tell you at breakfast."

Indy, Pete, and Ricky started the fire. Soon the aroma of sizzling bacon brought the girls outdoors with Blackie trotting beside them.

"How would you like your eggs? Sunny-side up or scrambled?" asked Ricky as he put butter in the skillet.

Blackie gave a woof and Holly laughed. "No eggs for you," she said. "I'll give you a bowl of canned milk."

Breakfast was not quite finished when the three gullers came marching up to the inn. They were not smiling.

"Uh-oh," Pam said. "Something's gone wrong."

"Will you have breakfast with us?" asked Emmy as Jane, Bill, and Gary came within hailing distance.

"We're not hungry," said Gary. "Just angry."

"Someone destroyed our gull-drying cages during the night," declared Jane. "The frames have been smashed and the wire ripped apart!"

"There's no use being here without cages," Bill said. "We might as well return to the mainland. When Sleepy Sam comes over today, ask if he can take us back with him."

"Who could have done such a mean thing?" said Emmy.

"I think it was Scally," Jane replied. All three told of seeing the *Witch* lingering offshore about daybreak.

"That rascal should be arrested!" Indy said. "And if he's guilty, we'll see to it that he is."

"But please don't go back now," Pam begged the gullers.

"If you do," Pete said, "you won't be in on the excitement when we catch these rascals."

Bill, who was sitting crossed-legged by the fire, looked up quickly. "Do you think you're really going to solve the mystery?"

"I think so," Pete said, "and soon, too."

At this the gullers cheered up and admitted their hunger. Ricky and Pete provided them with hearty breakfasts. Indy said he had some tools in the car. Together they could repair the gull cages and the young people could continue their work.

Bill managed a grin as he finished his meal and said, "I don't know what we'd do without you Hollisters."

After the skillet had been cleaned and the paper plates tossed into the fire, everyone trudged down the beach with Blackie scampering ahead. The wrecked gull cages lay some distance past the gullers' camp.

"The fellow dragged them here so we wouldn't hear him smash them," Gary said.

"Oh!" exclaimed Pam as she saw how twisted and broken the cages were.

"Don't worry, we can fix them," Indy said. He gave directions to Sue and Emmy to look for scraps of driftwood.

"We'll use those to splint the shattered wood," he explained.

Then the girls untwisted the wire, while Indy and the boys straightened bent nails with a hammer on a flat rock. Finally the broken frames were mended and the wire replaced. Although the cages looked a little bumpy here and there, they were usable once more.

"Now we can dry gulls again!" Jane said.

Bill turned to the visitors. "Indy, we certainly thank you," he said. "All of you have been a wonderful help."

Gary laughed and saluted. "The Audubon will carry on!"

"How about us?" Ricky asked. "What'll we do now?"

"Pam and I could go to the mainland and tell Cadwallader Clegg about Scally," Pete volunteered. Far down the beach the boy could see the clam

128

digger and his boat. "Maybe Sleepy Sam'll give us a ride over and back."

"All right," Emmy said, "but offer to pay."

"Who's going to watch the shack for the mystery man?" Holly asked.

"You, Ricky, and I," Indy replied.

"And Emmy and I'll build sand castles with Blackie," Sue declared as the two detective teams set off.

When Pete and Pam raced up to the clam digger he gave them a sleepy smile. But his face grew serious when Pam told him what they wanted.

"My boat's not for hire," he said, "but I'm always glad to give my friends a ride."

The children smiled and thanked him. After they helped load his clams into the skiff, Pete took an oar and they headed for the opposite shore. When they debarked at Cliffport, Sleepy Sam said he would wait until they returned.

The children walked off the dock toward the boat livery. It was open.

"Oh, look!" Pete said. "There's our boat—number twelve!"

The craft, which they had seen last on the sandy beach of Wicket-ee-nock, rocked in the waves alongside the catwalk.

"Come on," said Pete. "We're going to ask Mr. Scally some questions." As he led the way down the wooden stairs, Scally came out of the office.

"So there you are!" he scolded the children. "That's no way to take care of a boat!"

"What do you mean?" Pete replied. "It was stolen from Wicket-ee-nock."

"Don't tell me that story," Scally said with a frown. "The boat drifted to the mainland. You must have been careless with it."

"You gave us water instead of gasoline in that tin," Pam said hotly.

"You're dreaming," the unpleasant man replied.

"And what about the gull cages?" Pete asked accusingly. "Did you have anything to do with smashing them last night?"

"You'd better get out of here," Scally said menacingly. "Before I throw you in the drink."

Pete backed away from the threatening man and together the two children hustled up the stairs to the street.

"We'll report this to Cadwallader Clegg," Pete remarked to his sister as they walked away.

"Oh, wait," Pam said. "There's the library. Maybe they've received the book on heraldry."

The youngsters entered and Pam talked to the friendly librarian. The woman reached beneath the desk and pulled out a book which she handed to Pam. "Here you are," she said. "I think you'll find what you are looking for on page thirty."

A bookmark was in the place and Pam opened to it.

There was the same coat of arms that she had found on the beach.

Beneath was a caption that identified the ancient insignia as belonging to a royal Austrian family, noted for its fine horsemanship. To make sure, Pam took the illustration from her pocket and placed it alongside the picture in the book. They matched exactly.

"Thank you so much," Pam told the librarian as she returned the book. "This has been a real help."

"Don't you want to take it with you?"

"No, thank you," Pam replied, and the children hurried out.

As soon as they reached the sidewalk, they stopped. Pam's eyes flashed with excitement. "Pete! We're on the right track!" the girl exclaimed. "Austria is somehow tied up with this mystery. The coat of arms and the horses are Austrian and so is the man with the accent, I'll bet!"

"But how does it all fit together?" asked Pete as they hastened up the hill toward Cadwallader Clegg's house.

"I don't know, but it *must* somehow," Pam said, and mulled over all the clues.

This time they found Cadwallader Clegg at home.

"Welcome. Hello," he said. "How are things going on Wicket-ee-nock?"

"Not so good," Pete replied. The children quickly told him everything that had happened.

"So there really is a ghost horse, eh? I thought the gullers had seen one of the Lipizzaners," Cadwallader said, then added, "And Scally's acting rough, is he?"

Pete and Pam were not surprised to hear that the boat livery man had been in trouble off and on for a long time.

"I'm going to arrest him this time," Cadwallader declared, and snapped his suspenders so that his shiny badge jumped.

The one-man police force put on his jacket and marched down the hill with Pete and Pam.

"Where is the scoundrel?" Cadwallader asked as they neared the boat livery.

"I think he's inside," Pete said. "I'll go see."

The boy tiptoed down the steps and looked in the office door. Scally was on the telephone with his back to Pete. He was talking in an agitated voice.

"But they won't scare!" Scally declared. "How can we get it if we don't know where it is?"

The voice on the other end was so loud that even Pete could hear the reply. "You've done everything! Everything but find it. That's what you're getting paid for!"

Scally hung up, and wheeled about to see Pete peeking in the doorway. "So you're here again!" he thundered.

Cadwallader Clegg stepped up to block the doorway. "Scally, you're under arrest!" he said.

Scally looked frightened and glanced about the room, his eyes coming to rest on the open window.

"Scally, you're under arrest!"

Cadwallader Clegg reached around to his back pocket. A look of surprise came over his face. "Doggone!" he exclaimed. "Forgot to bring the handcuffs."

This made Scally sneer. "You're a great policeman," he taunted the officer. "Are you sure you know where the jail is?"

"Don't give me any sassy talk," Cadwallader Clegg said with authority. "You come with me, handcuffs or no."

Instead Scally backed toward the window.

"Don't you try to get away," Cadwallader warned him.

But the fellow retorted, "Come and get me!"

Both Cadwallader and Pete dashed forward, but Scally nimbly jumped out the window. He ran along the catwalk with Pete at his heels, and leaped into a motorboat!

CHAPTER 15

Secret in the Stove

As SCALLY bent to untie the rope, Pete reached over and grabbed his shirt. But the man wrenched away, nearly pulling the boy into the water. Then he started the motor and zipped away. Opening the throttle to full speed, Scally headed down the coast and soon was a mere pinpoint on the horizon.

"We'll get him yet," Cadwallader Clegg said. He returned to the boat livery office and telephoned the state police to be on the alert for Scally.

Pete and Pam thanked Cadwallader for his effort. "You'll let us know when the state police catch him, won't you?" asked Pete.

Cadwallader promised to do this and added that the Hollisters should be extra careful on Wicket-ee-nock in case the mean fellow returned.

"We'll have to go now," Pete said. "Sleepy Sam is waiting for us."

But first they stopped at the grocery and bought three large roast beef sandwiches, cold soda, and chocolate cupcakes.

As the children hurried along the pier, they waved to Captain Wade, who was cleaning up his ferryboat. "We'll have her running soon," the skipper called.

Sleepy Sam was ready and the youngsters climbed into the boat. The clam digger gave a big smile when he saw the lunch his passengers had brought. He and Pete took turns rowing and eating. While they all enjoyed the floating picnic, Pete and Pam discussed Scally's phone call. What was it that the man was being paid to find?

Pam thought that this thing might be at the bottom of the whole mystery. "I'll bet circus people aren't spying on the Franklins at all," she said.

Pete agreed. "And the brands on the horses are probably clues to the missing thing," he added. "Well, whatever Scally is up to, he wants to do it in secret. That's why he's trying to scare everybody off Wicket-ee-nock."

"With that corny ghost horse," said Pam.

"It is awful scary, though," Pete had to admit. "Where can Scally be keeping it?"

They asked Sleepy Sam if he had any idea where the horse could be hidden.

"No," was the reply. "I've never laid eyes on the thing myself, and I never want to. But Scally grew up around here, same as I did, and he knows every nook and cranny on the island." Then the clam digger rested on the oars and said earnestly, "You keep away from that Scally. He's no good. He might hurt you."

A few minutes later, Sleepy Sam beached his

rowboat. Pete and Pam hopped out. As they ran toward the inn, they saw Blackie straining at the rope which tied him to the porch. The dog was barking and whimpering.

"What's the matter, boy?" Pete asked, fondling him.

Blackie let out a few sharp barks and looked toward the back of the inn.

Pam held her hand over the dog's muzzle and listened. Not a sound. Pete tiptoed along the side of the building. Suddenly he heard a squeaky sound like a rusty hinge. Then came a scramble of footsteps.

His heart pounding with excitement, Pete raced around the corner of the inn in time to see the bearded man hurrying out the back door. He carried an armful of canned goods.

"Stop!" Pete cried out. This startled the intruder. He dropped several cans and dashed for the dunes. Pete chased after him but his foot hit one of the rolling cans and the boy went flying! He landed on his shoulder with such a thud that it stunned him for a moment.

"Are you hurt?" Pam cried, running over to her brother.

"Crickets! That was some spill!" Pete said ruefully, rising to his feet. "Where did that fellow go?"

"I don't know. He just seemed to disappear."

"He's somewhere in the dunes by now," Pam replied.

The boy went flying!

"Where did he come from?" asked Pam.

"The inn."

"Was it our food he was carrying?"

"I don't know," Pete said. "Let's look and see."

They hurried to the front and untied Blackie. Pam held the dog by his collar as they entered the house. Blackie sniffed about from one room to the other, finally stopping at the old cracked potbellied stove in the corner of the parlor. Pete lifted the lid and looked inside. A dozen cans of food lay among the ashes.

"Look at this," the boy exclaimed. "Beans, peaches, and French-fried potato sticks!"

So this was where the bearded stranger cached his supply of food! Pam reasoned that he must have lived in the inn before their arrival. No wonder the pump worked so easily!

"Then he hid his things in the stove and came back to get them when we weren't here," Pete added.

"I sort of feel sorry for him," Pam said kindly. "We put him out of his home."

"The fellow can survive a few more days," Pete remarked. "But we're bound to get him and Scally."

As Pete and Pam picked up the cans that the intruder had dropped, they talked about whether he and Scally were working together.

"Do you think they're both trying to scare us off the island?" Pete asked his sister as they set the canned goods alongside the outdoor fireplace.

At first Pam did not think so. "If that man we just saw were in league with Scally," she reasoned, "why would he risk coming here for his food?"

"That's right," Pete said. "Scally could supply him directly at the shack where he's been hiding."

"If the bearded man *is* the one who's hiding there," said Pam. "We're not certain he was the man in the yellow raincoat."

The children looked at each other, stumped.

Was the bearded man friend or foe? Was there one stranger or two on the island?

Whatever the truth should turn out to be, Pam felt sure that the man with the beard would supply an important link in their chain of clues.

"I wonder where the others have gone," said Pam as they entered the house again. Her question was answered immediately by a note, which she noticed for the first time, tacked to the doorway. It stated that Emmy and Sue had taken lunch to the stake-out team near the mysterious shack. "Let's go there right away," Pam suggested.

After Pete had tied Blackie to the porch again, they trudged across the dunes toward the ramshackle hut.

"Look," Pam said, pointing. "There they are!" The rest of the party were standing around the shack. As Pete and Pam ran over to join them, Ricky came out and said, "Everything is just as it was except that the sleeping bag is gone."

"I want to look too," Pam said. She stepped

in and came out saying that the cans of food were missing also.

"The poor fellow," Emmy remarked. "Now he must be sleeping outdoors and eating on the run."

Then Pete and Pam told about the bearded man at the inn.

"Maybe two men are camping out," Holly said.

"I've got a hunch there's only one," declared Indy. "And I'd like to know what he's doing on the island."

Quickly Pete and Pam told of their adventures with Scally and Cadwallader. "The bearded man and Scally may be looking for the same thing," Pete concluded. "If we could only catch one of them and find out!"

As the adventurers walked back to the Lobster Inn, they decided to scour the island for the foreigner.

"We can go out when it's dark," Pete suggested, "and look for a campfire."

"We have to keep an eye on that shack and the inn too," Ricky spoke up.

"We'll do it all tonight," Indy said, "but you'll have to wait for me to come back from the Franklins' house." Pete and Pam learned that while they were in Cliffport, Mrs. Franklin had invited Sue, Emmy, and Indy to visit that evening.

After supper the older children volunteered to tidy up and the others set off immediately. Then, as the light began to fade from the western sky, Pete spotted Jane racing along the beach. She was carrying an unlit flare. When she reached them she said breathlessly that she and Bill had seen two men running up the beach on the ocean side of Wicket-ee-nock.

"One might be the fellow we're looking for!" Pete exclaimed. "Let's go!"

They raced inside for flashlights. Then, taking Blackie with them, the Hollisters and Jane set off across the island and soon were on the seaward shore. It was dusk, but far down the beach they could make out Bill and Gary hurrying toward them.

"Did you see anybody?" Bill asked as the youths reached the Hollister party.

"No," replied Pete.

Bill said that he and Jane had not seen the men's faces. "By the time I went back to camp to get Gary," he added, "they had disappeared."

It was decided that the prowlers were probably somewhere between the gullers' camp and the cliff.

Pete said, "Jane, why don't you go with Bill and Gary and search from here south? The rest of us will go north."

The gullers agreed, and Jane handed Ricky the flare. "Use this in case you need help," she said. "Just scratch the tip of it on a rock."

"Will you be safe enough?" Gary asked as the children started away.

"We'll be okay with Blackie here," Pete replied. With that the youngsters fanned out and walked slowly toward the cliff, scanning the ground for footprints.

Blackie ranged around in great circles. "Come on, boy," Pete urged him. "Pick up the trail!"

Half an hour later, moonlight bathed the beach. When Blackie barked sharply, Pam ran over to see him pawing behind a low boulder. Then she heard a groan. "Pete, come here quick!" she called.

The three others raced to her side.

"It's a man and he's hurt!" Pam said, pointing to a figure lying face-down in the shadow of the rock.

Pete gently turned the man over and all gasped at once. It was the bearded stranger. He was unconscious.

With hands trembling, Ricky scratched the tip of the flare on the rock. It flamed into action, sending ball after ball of colored light high into the night sky.

Soon shouts were heard and Indy and Mr. Franklin came racing over the dunes toward them. The gullers dashed up the beach. Pam, meanwhile, scooped up some sea water and splashed it on the fellow's whiskery face. The man's eyes fluttered open. He moaned again as Pete and Indy propped him against the boulder.

"Who are you?" Pam asked.

"Nicklas. My name is Nicklas," came the reply in a heavy German accent.

"You're an Austrian, I'll bet," Pam continued.

"Why—how did you know that?" the man asked in surprise.

Then he moaned again and held his head. Ricky flashed his light, which revealed a large bump on the side of Mr. Nicklas' forehead. The man said that he had fallen and hit his head on the rock. "I was chasing after a fellow named Scally," he explained. "I wanted to question him."

"Scally?" Pete asked, looking puzzled. "Why?"

"Because I'm a detective," came the reply. Now it was the listeners' turn to be amazed.

"A detective!" Pete exclaimed. "We're detectives, too."

"I thought you might be," Mr. Nicklas said with a wry smile. He explained that he had come from Austria to Wicket-ee-nock Island on a special mission.

"Like what?" Mr. Franklin spoke up.

"I can't tell you."

"But you'll have to," Pam said. "Otherwise we'll never solve the mystery of this island."

"It seems to me," Gary said to the stranger, "that you're part of the puzzle."

"Believe me," the man declared, "I'm a detective and I'm looking for something very important."

"Is that why you wanted to scare us off the island?" asked Bill.

"I'm not trying to scare anybody," Mr. Nicklas replied. "Please believe me."

"Then what are you hunting for?" Pam said.

144

"Please tell us." Gently she patted some cool water on his bump.

The man sighed. "*Ach!* Very well," he said. "I am hunting for a coat of arms stolen from Vienna."

"A coat of arms! What's so important about that?" asked Pete.

"You don't understand," Mr. Nicklas said, gesturing with his hands. "This coat of arms is made of jewels."

CHAPTER 16

The Hidden Door

THE Hollisters were amazed to hear about the jeweled coat of arms and Pam said, "Is this a picture of it?" She pulled the colored illustration from her pocket and Nicklas looked surprised.

"Where did you get that?" the Austrian detective asked.

Pam told him about finding the piece of paper on the beach.

"Yes, I lost it," Nicklas said. He explained that he had brought the picture from Europe in order to identify the stolen coat of arms.

At this point Ricky asked if Nicklas had credentials.

"Indeed, yes!" replied the man. With Indy and Bill's help he stood up unsteadily, then pulled out his wallet. He showed an identification card, written in German, which Mr. Franklin was able to read.

"This proves you are a private detective from Vienna," the horse trainer said, then added curiously, "You've come a long way to solve this mystery."

"Ah yes," replied the Viennese, "but the coat of arms is very valuable. It was stolen from the castle of a former prince and he has employed me to get it back again."

"Do you know who took it?" Pam asked.

"Yes, Max Stein," was the reply.

"We know that name!" Pete exclaimed. "That's the groom who brought the horses to America, isn't it, Mr. Franklin?"

The trainer nodded. "Several months ago I saw the Lipizzaners at the prince's stable," he explained. "My wife and I were playing with a European circus at the time. When we got back here we decided to buy the horses. Stein delivered them and was supposed to stay a week to help the animals get used to their new home. Instead he left after several days."

"Yes," the detective said. "The ferry captain told me that he cleared out just a few hours before I came. Stein knew I was on his heels. He spotted me in New York and gave me the slip."

"Do our police have his description?" asked Pete.

Despite his painful bump, the Austrian smiled. "I wired it to them as soon as the theft was discovered. I am not worried. Your police are very efficient. They will pick him up. What I have to do now is find the coat of arms. It must be here on the island."

"I should think he'd take it with him," Jane remarked, and the other gullers nodded.

"No," the detective said. "The insignia is too hard to carry. It is almost two feet high and very heavy. Besides, Stein will not risk being caught with it. I am sure he plans to return for it later."

147

As soon as the detective said that the coat of arms was on the island, Pete and Pam had exchanged excited looks.

"That must be what Scally is looking for!" Pete exclaimed. Quickly he told Nicklas about Scally's telephone call and escape.

The Austrian snapped his fingers. "So!" he exclaimed. "I suspected that fellow was after the treasure!" Then he closed one eye and nodded his head thoughtfully. "I think I know where Scally is hiding." He pointed down the coast to the rocky cliff. "He is probably in one of the caves," the Austrian went on. "I was chasing him in that direction when I fell."

"Then let's go get him!" exclaimed Ricky.

"Too late," Mr. Franklin spoke up. "The tide is high."

"Yikes, we can climb down the cliff from the top," Ricky declared. "Let's go!"

"Wait," said Pete. "Maybe it's better not to catch Scally yet."

As Ricky looked puzzled, the detective smiled. "I see your point," he said to Pete. "By now Scally may have learned where the treasure is. He could lead us to it."

"There are brands on the Lipizzaners," Holly told the detective excitedly. "Maybe they are clues to the hiding place."

"Perhaps Mr. Nicklas was the one who was getting into the barn at night to examine them," Indy suggested.

148

Nicklas looked surprised. "No, indeed," he replied. "I am beginning to think you children know more about this mystery than I do."

Quickly Pete told him about the odd brands.

Then Pam, who had been waiting to ask an important question, spoke up. "Mr. Nicklas, were you the one living in the old shack in the dune?"

"Yes," he replied.

"Then you were the man who kept our boat from crashing into the cliff?"

"That's right. I tried to help you. I left the warning note because I was afraid Scally would hurt you."

"How about the time you waved us off?" Pete asked.

"I thought Scally was in the caves," the detective replied. He explained that he had intended to search there the evening Pete had tried to follow him down the cliff. "You made me change my plans," he added with a smile.

On further questioning the boy learned that Nicklas was not the man Pam had seen slithering over the sand dune, nor was he one of the two who had prowled the inn with flashlights.

"You poor man," Pam sympathized. "I guess we chased you out of the inn, didn't we?"

Nicklas smiled. "Yes. Luckily I found the shack to live in."

"And then we chased you out of there, too," said Pam. As she spoke she noticed that the detective's shoulders were drooping. "We'd better take you back to the inn to rest now," she added.

"That's right," agreed Indy. "I'll bet you need a good hot meal, too. My sister will fix it for you. She should be back at the inn by now."

"We'll sound the alert," declared Ricky. He and Holly raced away, flashlights bobbing, to tell Emmy.

Then the gullers said good night and headed for their camp. By the time the rest of the party arrived at the inn, the Indian woman had clam chowder bubbling in the pot while bacon and eggs sizzled in a skillet. Nicklas was introduced and the girls served him at once.

As the hungry man began to eat, Mr. Franklin told him that he and his wife would watch the caves and report when Scally came out and where he went. "He'll be mighty wet, I can tell you that," said the horse trainer with a grim chuckle. Then he added, "My wife will be glad to hear that this mystery is not about circus spies."

As Mr. Franklin strode away into the darkness, the Hollisters began to tell Nicklas all that had happened.

"Ah yes," he said when they had finished, "you are truly detectives. And you, dear lady," he told Emmy, "are an excellent cook." Putting down his empty plate, he gave a contented sigh. "I am glad we have finally met."

"Why did you avoid us?" Pete asked.

"Scally saw me spying on him," he replied. "I

did not want him to see us together, for fear that he would make trouble for you, too."

The detective fell silent and the children saw the faraway look come into his eyes.

"Scally is not smart enough to think of the ghost horse himself," he said softly. "The man he works for must have done that. *Who can he be?*"

"Maybe Stein is that Scally-wag's boss," Holly spoke up.

"No," Pete objected. He pointed out that Scally had been looking for the treasure over two weeks. If Stein had ordered him to get it, he would have told the boat livery man where he had hidden it.

The detective leaned toward them, his eyes gleaming earnestly in the firelight. "My friends, we must be very careful. I'm afraid the boss is a dangerous fellow—and we don't know who he is."

"Yet!" said Holly. "Good night," she added sleepily, and went inside to slip into bed with Sue, so that her cot could be removed for the detective.

In the morning at breakfast Sue was introduced to the visitor from Vienna.

"Nikky is a nice name," said the little girl as she shook the detective's hand.

"Mr. Nicklas," Emmy corrected her gently. "You must be respectful."

"That is all right," said the detective, patting Sue's dark hair. "My friends at home call me Nikky. I would like all of you to do so, too."

As the children beamed delightedly, Pam suddenly exclaimed, "Oh—I almost forgot!" She ran inside and came out with the yellow rain hat. "Thank you for warning us, Nikky," she said as she returned it.

While they were finishing breakfast, Mr. Franklin came and sat wearily on the porch steps.

"Scally's given us the slip," he said. "My wife and I took turns watching the caves last night, but he never came out. Finally, at daybreak, I went in and looked. He was gone."

"Maybe he didn't hide there after all," Pete said.

"Or he knows a secret way out," Pam suggested.

Mr. Franklin thought that could be and told them that the cliff was honeycombed with cracks and holes.

The detective rose briskly and said that they would go over to search the rocks at once. "We can look for Scally and the treasure at the same time," he declared.

The horse trainer had work to do and headed for his barn. All the others except Sue and Emmy hurried eagerly toward the cliff. Even Blackie barked with excitement as they trotted across the dunes toward the ocean shore. They saw the gullers in the distance and waved to them, but hastened on to the cliff.

The tide was out and they climbed at once to the rock ledge in front of the caves.

Indy, the girls, and Blackie went into one, while the rest of the party entered the other. The boys and Nikky found themselves in a large gloomy chamber with smooth rock walls. A search revealed no cracks or holes for escape.

Outside they found the other explorers waiting.

"I guess you had no luck either," said Pam when she saw the boys' faces.

For several hours they climbed among the crags, looking into crevices and holes.

Once they heard a small voice crying, "Hello." They looked up to see Sue and Emmy waving from the cliff top.

A little later Holly shouted, "Look!" and pointed down into a wide cleft between a slab of rock and the base of the cliff. "There's a rowboat!"

"I know," called the detective. "It is mine. I keep it hidden there."

Holly looked disappointed and they went on searching. At noon they were about to give up when Blackie, who was climbing directly in front of Pam, wriggled through a small hole and disappeared.

"Blackie, come back!" Pam called. She put her ear to the opening and the dog barked. The sound echoed and re-echoed.

"Come here, everybody!" Pam cried. "Blackie has found a hollow place!"

Ricky wriggled inside. Moments later he stuck his head out of the hole and exclaimed, "There's a stairway in here and it leads up!"

Accidentally Ricky banged his head on the long rock above him. It tilted up, leaving an opening big enough to walk into!

"There's a stairway in here!"

"Crickets!" Pete cried out. "A balancing rock! That's using your head, Ricky!"

"No wonder I didn't find this entrance," Nikky said.

"Yikes! Who could have made this passage?" Ricky wondered. Indy thought that perhaps it had been the work of pirates many years before.

Not waiting to speculate further about the secret entrance, the Hollisters filed in, followed by Indy and Nikky. Dim light came from a small hole high in the rock wall. A bird flew in and out. When Blackie barked again, Pam put a hand around his muzzle and they walked quietly up the uneven stone steps.

At the top, Pete found a wooden door. It would not push or pull so Pete tried to slide it. It moved quietly to the right, and the searchers found themselves looking directly into one of the horse stalls.

Amos Franklin, standing in the middle of the ring with the two Lipizzaners, looked amazed. His lips moved but he could say nothing. Finally he walked over to the sleuths as they entered the barn.

"I can't believe it!" he whispered hoarsely. "How did you get in here?"

Pam explained what had happened. The horse trainer was so surprised that for a minute he could only shake his head. As he watched, Pete slid the door shut. Then he found a tiny latch at the side of the stall, which he could trip with his finger to open the panel again.

"So that is how the prowler managed," Indy said.

"But first he banged the barn door to make us think he went out that way," Ricky added.

Then Nikky knelt down and examined the brands on Franz and Josef. Finally he rose again. "But what can they mean?" he mused. "The crescent and star. Does the Turkish symbol have something to do with this?"

"One thing is sure," Indy declared. "If Scally *does* know where the treasure is, he'll act fast."

"I think so, too," Pete said. "We must try to pick up his trail without letting him know it."

"Please be very careful," Mr. Franklin said.

"We'll take care," Pam promised him. She said that they ought to leave the way they came so no one would know they had found the secret passageway.

The searchers filed out the back of the stall, closed the panel, and felt their way down the stone steps, with Blackie flopping along behind them. They stepped through the opening in the cliff and stood blinking in the sun.

As Pete closed the stone door, Pam said, "I'll bet Scally was hiding in there last night. That's why the Franklins didn't see him come out of the cave."

While they made their way down over the rocks, Pete considered the possibility that the ghost horse could have been hidden in the rock chamber. "It would be too hard for the animal to climb up there," he decided as he joined the others on the beach.

That afternoon the Hollisters and Nikky partitioned the island into four sections, then divided up the sleuths, young and old, to comb each part. But they all returned at suppertime with no sign of Scally, the ghost horse, Turkish symbols, or anything else that looked like the brand on the Lipizzaners.

When darkness fell, Indy was about to douse the bonfire, but Holly begged Emmy to tell them a bedtime stroy.

"Once there was an Indian maiden in the mountains of New Mexico," Emmy began. "She had a beautiful shell necklace. Then one dark, moonless night—" She stopped short as everyone was startled by the sound of rapid hoofbeats on the beach.

"The ghost horse!" Sue cried out, and flung her arms about Emmy.

"Maybe it's one of the Lipizzaners," Pete said.

"Then we have to catch him," Pam cried out, and ran toward the shore.

"Wait, don't go!" Pete called, and raced after his sister. The others hurried close behind them.

"It is the ghost horse!" Pam screamed as the animal bore down upon the astounded group. On the back of the small steed was a rider dressed in a black cloak, which he held across his face.

Pete and Indy poised themselves to spring at the rider. But Blackie saved them the trouble. The brave little dog dashed in front of the galloping horse, yapping furiously. The animal reared and whinnied. The rider fell off backward onto the sand.

"Catch him! Catch him!" Pete cried out. All of them made a dash for the struggling figure cloaked in black.

CHAPTER 17

The Witch

THE unseated rider rolled over and over on the sandy beach, then sprang to his feet and dashed into the darkness before anyone could lay a hand on him.

"That slippery eel!" exclaimed Indy.

"Look!" Ricky cried. "I've caught the horse!" The dingy white animal stood meekly while Ricky held the rope in his hand. The long horn had slipped from the horse's head and now was slung under his neck like a huge ice-cream cone.

"We knew it wasn't a real horn," Pam said as she examined it. "See, it's made of papier-mâché."

"Crickets, wait! What's this?" Pete said as he led the horse to the front of the Lobster Inn. There the firelight flickered on the halter rope. *It had red dye on one end!*

"The rope that Scally took from us!" Pam declared. "Now we can prove he was in the plot."

"What a villain," Emmy said tersely.

"I'd like to get my hands on him," Indy growled. "He's a real troublemaker." Then he grinned and scooped Blackie into his arms. "And you're a brave fellow," he said, hugging his pet.

"Blackie's a detective, too," Holly spoke up. "He discovered the secret passage."

The spaniel trotted proudly to the fireplace with

Indy, and the others followed. Meanwhile, Pete tethered the horse to the porch of the inn, then sat down beside Blackie. As he stroked the dog's ears, the boy grinned.

"I'm glad the ghost horse showed up tonight," he declared. "Now we know that Scally and his boss have not found the treasure. If they had, they wouldn't have tried to scare us again."

"Oh, where can that coat of arms be?" Pam asked. "Think, everybody!"

As the firelight flicked on and off their troubled faces, the children offered one theory after another. But none really fit the clues on the horses.

"If we only knew what the brands stood for," Pete said. "What is crescent-shaped beside the Turkish symbol?"

"The moon," said Holly.

Ricky snorted. "The treasure's not on the moon," he declared.

Suddenly Sue jumped up. "Listen to my words," she cried shrilly.

The little girl's voice had been drowned out by those of her brothers and sisters, and Emmy said, "Yes, let's listen to Sue."

The four-year-old sighed, yawned, and rubbed her eyes sleepily. Then she clung to Emmy and looked up into the woman's face.

"Come on, dear," Emmy said. "What would you like to tell us?"

"Nick-nack Island is like the moon."

"Yikes," Ricky said in a low voice, "Sue must be asleep already."

"No, I'm not," his sister retorted. "Our island is shaped just like the moon. Isn't it, Emmy?" She yawned again and leaned against the woman.

"Oh, my goodness!" exclaimed Emmy. "She's right! I hardly noticed at the time, because I was so busy watching all of you."

"Slow down, now," said Indy. "What do you mean?"

"This morning," his sister explained, "when Sue and I were on the cliff top, the tide was all the way out. We could see the ends of the island that are usually covered by water. They curve into the ocean like the tips of a crescent."

As Emmy picked up Sue and cradled the dozing youngster in her arms, Pam's face glowed with excitement. "Sue has solved the mystery of the crescent brand!"

"And the star could mean the location of the treasure," Pete chimed in, "—offshore, midway between the curving tips of the island."

"That's right by the cliff!" cried Holly.

Everyone was excited except Sue, whose angelic face, with closed eyes, rested against Emmy's shoulder.

"Ah, now I see it," Nikky said, putting a finger to his forehead. "The other brand you mentioned, like a pyramid, could be a buoy, maybe, or an old lighthouse?"

"But there isn't any," Ricky said.

Just then Blackie whimpered and sniffed into the darkness cloaked about them.

"Let's speak lower," Indy warned them.

"Yes," Holly said, "'cause Scally-wag might be listening out there."

"Well, what's the next thing we should do, young detectives?" Indy asked softly.

"First, go to bed," Emmy interrupted as she stood up with Sue.

"And the next thing," said Pam, following them, "is to locate that treasure."

After the rest had gone inside, Pete and the men decided to stand guard all night in case Scally returned to get his horse.

"I'll take first watch," the boy volunteered. Indy and Nikky were to follow in that order.

Sitting on the porch of Lobster Inn, Pete looked and listened. He was too excited to be sleepy, but when Indy spelled him, the boy went inside, rolled on his cot, and was soon fast asleep.

He was awakened next morning by the laughter of his brother and sisters.

The blond boy dressed and walked outdoors into the sunlight. There stood a young man with a pleasant smile, surrounded by the other youngsters.

"Guess who it is!" Ricky shouted and did a handspring.

Suddenly a look of recognition came into Pete's eyes. He grinned broadly. "Why—Nikky, it's you! What happened to your beard?"

"Let's speak lower," Indy warned them.

"Sue wanted me to shave it off this morning," the Austrian detective replied. "She said it tickled her when she hugged me."

Out of the corner of his eye, Pete saw that Emmy was looking admiringly at the clean-shaven Nikky. "Goodness," she said. "How young you look."

"Please leave your beard off permanently," Pam begged him.

"Maybe I'll do that," Nikky replied, stroking his chin.

"Well, who's for breakfast?" Emmy asked gaily. When the meal was over, Holly ran down to the shore to hail Sleepy Sam as he arrived to dig clams.

"Guess what happened! Guess what happened!" Holly cried, jumping up and down on the sand. With a bucket in one hand and a shovel in the other, Sleepy Sam followed the bubbling youngster to Lobster Inn. There he was told all about the excitement of the night before.

"Do you know who owns this horse?" Indy asked Sleepy Sam.

The clam digger looked at the animal closely with droopy eyelids. He peered at the front and the back and then the legs of the skinny horse.

"You do know whose it is," Pam said.

"'Course I do. Thelma belongs to me."

"It's your horse?" Ricky asked, wrinkling his nose.

"Yup. Somebody made off with her about a month ago. Where ya been, Thelma, poor girl?"

Nikky smiled to see the show of affection as Sleepy Sam stroked the nose of his lost horse.

The clam digger unhitched Thelma and walked her to a patch of high grass near the edge of a dune. "Eat hearty," he said. "I'll get you some water."

"Yikes," Ricky said. "Now we have to find out how Thelma got on Wicket-ee-nock."

"First, we have to search for the treasure," Pete declared.

When they were ready to start, Pete called to the clam digger, who was helping Thelma to a long drink of water from his bucket. "Sleepy Sam, was there ever a lighthouse or a buoy on the ocean side of Wicket-ee-nock?"

"No—just a small signal light."

"There was!" Pete exclaimed, running over to the clam digger. "What did it look like?"

"Like this," Sleepy Sam replied, putting the bucket on the ground. He held his hands in the shape of a pyramid.

The others all crowded about.

"Now the whole thing's beginning to make sense!" Pam said. "And Sue, you found the answer." She hugged her sister as the clam digger continued to tell about the old signal light. It had been a hollow pyramid made of rocks with a round light on top to warn ships away from the shoals and sand bars.

"But a hurricane knocked it down," Sleepy Sam said. "You can still see the remains of it at low tide. It's just about two inches above the water."

"Wowee!" Holly cried out. "How long will we have to wait for low tide, Sleepy Sam?"

"About two hours."

"Crickets!" exclaimed Pete. "I'll bet the treasure is hidden in that rock base!"

Ricky's face was red with excitement. "Yikes! Only two more hours and we'll have it!"

But there was one thought which crossed Pam's mind like a storm cloud. *What if Scally also knew about the old light? Suppose he had overheard them talking the night before?* She mentioned her worry, and Nikky looked serious.

"I think we had better find that fellow right away," he said. "We don't want trouble with him when we go for the treasure."

Again the searchers divided into teams. The lower end of the island was assigned to Pam, Holly, and Emmy. The Indian woman was to leave Sue and Blackie with Mrs. Franklin and then join the girls. The middle section, including the rocky cliff, was left to the two men.

"If you sight Scally," Indy told the children, "send one member of your team to tell us. The others stay hidden and watch him."

"Ricky and I'll take the northern part of the island," Pete said.

"If he's on Wicket-ee-nock, we'll find him," the redhead declared.

166

He and Pete trotted off along the beach. As they passed the Franklins' place, Pete wondered what new tricks the horse trainers were practicing that day. But his thoughts left the Lipizzaners as he and Ricky came onto the bare wide beach which stretched to the rocks at the tip of the island.

Ricky stopped suddenly and pointed ahead. "What's that, Pete? Do you see something out there?"

Pete shielded his eyes from the blaze of the morning sun and squinted. "Something dark on the shore."

"And I thought I saw someone run across the beach into the dunes," Ricky said. Without another word, both boys raced toward the end of the island.

"Crickets!" Pete cried as they drew closer. "It's a boat!"

As they ran along the water's edge, the boat appeared larger and larger until finally Pete stopped short. The black lettering on the bow now stood out clear and sharp against the white paint. It said, "THE WITCH."

"What are we waiting for?" Ricky said impatiently, pulling Pete by the arm.

"Take it easy," his older brother said. "Suppose Scally's on there and he catches us—how could we tell the others? We've got to be very quiet."

"Yikes, I didn't think of that."

Crouching low, the brothers ran along the

beach to the shadow of the boat. With the tide receding, the *Witch* lay half on the sand, half in the water.

Pete leaped up, grabbed the edge of the boat, and quietly hoisted himself onto the deck. Then he reached down and helped Ricky aboard. The two boys stood still and listened. Not a sound.

Pete took a step forward to look into the large open hatch in the stern. The bottom was strewn with hay, and a horse's feed bag lay in one corner.

A cold tingling ran up and down the boy's spine. *This is where the ghost horse had been hidden.*

Ricky gulped and looked at Pete. "Poor old Thelma had a boat ride every night Scally tried to scare us," he whispered.

"And to think the horse might have been hidden right here the morning we spied Scally and the *Witch* on the sand bar," Pete said softly.

Ricky quivered at the mention of Scally. He whispered, "Do you think he's here?"

Pete held a finger to his lips. "We'll know soon enough," he replied. Tiptoeing cautiously, the brothers searched every part of the boat. Nobody was aboard. Even the small cabin was empty.

Ricky mopped his forehead with the palm of his hand. "Phew. Now I feel better."

"But we must hurry back and tell the others right away," Pete said.

The boys stepped out of the cabin and were

halfway across the deck when suddenly a raucous noise sounded behind them. A voice said, "Scally, are you there?"

Pete and Ricky froze with fright!

CHAPTER 18

An Unexpected Catch

"SCALLY, where are you? Do you hear me? Answer me at once!" The words were punctuated with static.

Not knowing what to expect, Pete whirled about. The cabin was still empty, but the words continued to blare forth over the boat's two-way radio.

"Scally, I can't hear you," said the voice, "but get this message. Double-check on the zero hour. I'll be there. We have to be quick about it. The Hollisters are too hot. Over and out."

"Yikes! What'll we do now?" asked Ricky.

"Same as before. Go back and report. I'll bet that was Scally you saw racing away from the boat. He must have seen us coming."

"But where is he now?" Ricky said, glancing uneasily toward the dunes.

"I'll bet he's on his way to the signal light. Come on, let's hurry!"

"Wait! Suppose he comes back. One of us should stay and watch like Indy said."

"It's getting too late," the older boy replied. "He won't be back. Come on!"

The boys climbed the rail, jumped to the sand, then raced along the beach as fast as they could.

"Wait! Wait!" Ricky cried. Pete stopped to let

his brother catch his breath. "Pete—do you suppose—that voice was the boss?"

As they started trotting again, Pete replied, "Yes. It sounded like the man Pam and I heard talking to Scally over the telephone." Pete lengthened his stride, and wondered who the fellow could be.

The running boys stayed close to the shoreline and headed for the base of the cliff.

By the time they reached it, the tide had gone out enough so that they could skirt the boulders on the wet sand.

"Indy! Nikky!" Ricky shouted as he spied two figures down the beach a way.

The men halted. Pete and Ricky pounded up to them, and poured out their story.

"I'll go tell the others," Indy offered, and hurried away.

The boys and Nikky eyed the receding water with worried looks.

"Scally must be hiding around here, somewhere," Pete declared. The three searched amongst the dunes on both sides of the cliff and the rocks in front of it. There was no sign of the rival treasure hunter.

"Maybe he's covered himself with sand," Ricky suggested, then exclaimed, "Look! Here come the others!"

In a few minutes all the islanders, with the exception of the Franklins and Sue, stood at the foot of the cliff, anxiously watching the tide go out.

"I wish we knew exactly where the signal light was," Nikky remarked, looking at the wide expanse of surf before the cliff. "Every minute's going to count."

"I wonder if Scally has it spotted," Ricky said.

"I'm afraid so," replied Pete, and told them that the ruffian had known the island since boyhood.

Tensely Pam looked seaward. With every wash of the waves she hoped to glimpse the top of the old light.

Holly climbed onto one of the rocks and gazed out over the ocean.

"There's a boat," she said, "and it's coming this way."

A small motorboat churned slowly toward the island in the shallow water. The man at the wheel was bent so low that only the top of his head could be seen.

Then suddenly, without warning, a sandy mound on the beach north of the rocks burst open. Up jumped Scally! The prowler dashed along the wet flats toward the motorboat.

"He's heading for the light!" Pete cried out.

Everyone leaped in pursuit. But Scally was well out into the shallow water. As his long legs ate up the distance, he called out, "Closer, come closer!" The man in the motorboat obeyed.

"He'll ground it, if he doesn't look out," Pam thought. "Oh, I hope he does!"

Suddenly Pete groaned as he saw Scally reach

down into the water. "Oh, he had the place pin-pointed, all right!" the boy thought. Scally's arm thrashed out. Then he seemed to grasp hold of something and a moment later he pulled out a package wrapped in oilskin.

"Stop! Halt! Get him!" the young voices cried out as Scally splashed toward the waiting motor-boat.

Indy and Nikky jumped on the fugitive. But he was quick enough to flip the package into the boat. The motor roared and churned, making the green-ish water turn white as whipped cream.

As the craft gained headway, Pete and Bill leaped together for the gunwale. They grabbed hold and jerked, tipping the motorboat! Pete glanced up at the man who tumbled into the wa-ter. He could hardly believe what he saw—the Snowman!

As Bill and Gary seized the splashing fellow, Pete grabbed for the oilskin package. The dripping captives were herded ashore, while Emmy and Jane, with the rest of the youngsters, towed the boat up onto the sand. There the detectives looked over their shivering prisoners.

"So you're behind all this," Pete said accusingly to the ice-cream man.

The fellow's plump face was flushed and his little black eyes sparkled angrily. "No, it was Scally."

"He lies," the other man shot back. "I was working for him!"

"Stop! Halt! Get him!"

All watched breathlessly while Nikky opened the oilskin package and uncovered the coat of arms! The two horse heads were made of sparkling diamonds, and the rest of the ancient insignia was covered with gold leaf and rubies.

"Yikes! It must be worth a million!" Ricky blurted.

"And it would have been all mine," the Snowman growled, "if it weren't for you Hollisters."

"Save your story," Indy said. "We're taking you to Cadwallader Clegg!"

Scally's eyes darted about, as if he were looking for a chance to escape. But Indy and Gary held him tightly.

Halfway across the island, they were surprised to see a party of men approaching.

"The police!" Ricky cried. "State troopers!"

"With Cadwallader Clegg and Sleepy Sam, too!" exclaimed Pam.

"Well, you beat us to it," Cadwallader declared, striding up to them. He turned to Scally. "We have handcuffs this time!" The state troopers manacled the prisoners, then marched them off to the dock, where Captain Wade's ferryboat waited.

"Ricky," Indy said, "run get Sue and the Franklins. We'll all go along!"

In fifteen minutes the *Mermaid* was plowing toward Cliffport with everyone gathered in the bow. The bedraggled prisoners sat on a bench between two troopers, while Blackie barked at them and excited questions filled the air.

"Now quiet, everybody," boomed Cadwallader Clegg. "We're going to get some answers here!"

"First," Indy said, "tell us how you knew where Scally was."

"The state police intercepted messages which he and the Snowman were sending on their two-way radios," Cadwallader replied.

"We found the Snowman's radio in the bottom of his ice-cream cart," a trooper said.

"We thought you were a nice man," Sue piped up sadly, looking at the Snowman.

The culprit looked glumly at the deck.

"Listen"—Scally spoke up quickly—"I'll talk, if you go easy on me."

At this the Snowman looked up. "I'll tell it myself," he said bitterly. "I don't want to be blamed for more than my share."

Then the facts came out. The Snowman, whose real name was Tink Luden, was a petty criminal from a big city. He was also Stein's cousin. When the Austrian groom had seen Nikky on his trail in New York, he realized that he must hide the coat of arms and make his getaway. He decided the safest place for the treasure would be on the island. He called Tink and told him that after he had found a hiding place, he would brand clues to it on the horses.

Mr. Franklin looked puzzled. "Why didn't he just hide a note or tell you the location in a letter?"

"Max was afraid to write the secret down," Tink replied, "for fear someone else might see the letter. Max was pretty nervous by then," he added scornfully, and told them that Stein had fled to another big city, where Tink was to meet him with the jeweled insignia.

The ice-cream vendor gave the groom's address as a state trooper wrote it down.

Nikky grinned. "Now Stein can be nervous in jail," he said.

"But you never intended to turn over the coat of arms to your cousin, did you?" Pete asked.

"Of course not," replied the Snowman. He explained that he had used the ice-cream business for a front. "I hired Scally to help me," he went on, "because he knew the island well."

"But there were too many people around," put in Scally, "so Tink thought up the ghost horse to scare them away."

"And that's when you stole my poor Thelma," Sleepy Sam said, and shook his fist at the prisoners.

"Scally took the horse," the Snowman said quickly, "and he's the one who rode it." Tink explained that the *Witch*, with Thelma aboard, was usually hidden in a cove on the mainland.

Scally glared at the children and Blackie growled. As Pam grabbed the dog's collar, she said, "I guess it was the two of you who searched the inn."

"Of course," said the Snowman. "I had to find out your name before I could send the telegram. Scally spied on you the first night, but he didn't learn anything. The only thing he did right was to smash the cages."

"We saw you slithering over the top of the dune," Pam said to the ruffian, "but where did you go? We found your footprints leading into the ocean."

"Tink was waiting for me just offshore," Scally replied.

"I told him to walk the ghost horse into the water, too," the boss put in. "I had to do all the thinking for Scally."

His companion's eyes narrowed with anger. "I showed you the secret stairs! And if you're so smart, why didn't you figure out the brands on the horses? You'd never have known what they meant if I hadn't eavesdropped on the Hollisters!"

For a moment everyone sat silent, looking at the miserable prisoners.

"Any more questions?" asked Cadwallader Clegg.

"Yes," shouted a voice from the wheelhouse. It was Captain Wade. "Which one of those two pried open the seam in my boat?"

"Scally did," said the Snowman. "I told him to disable it, so nobody could go over to the island. I didn't think the old tub would sink."

"That was a big mistake," said Cadwallader.

"It kept the Hollisters on Wicket-ee-nock Island!"
He chuckled at the thought.

By now the *Mermaid* was close to Cliffport and
the passengers could see three police cars and a
group of townspeople waiting on the dock.

Captain Wade reached up and pulled the boat
whistle twice, and the ferry nosed into the slip.

"I'll see you tonight on the island," Nikky
promised the Hollisters, and hastened off with the
police and prisoners. Moments later the cars roared
away.

Then the islanders and Sleepy Sam returned to
Wicket-ee-nock on the ferryboat.

"We owe you so much," Mr. Franklin said to
the Hollisters when they were once again on
shore. "Now we can work in peace with our
horses."

"And we can finish our job, too," declared Bill.

Then Sleepy Sam spoke up. "Somethin' I forgot to tell you." He tilted back his hat and stood
up very straight. "Cadwallader Clegg has put me
in charge of a giant clambake to be given tonight
right in front of the old Lobster Inn."

The children whooped and clapped. But Ricky
was not quite so happy as the others. He went
over to Emmy and whispered in her ear, "But you
promised me."

"What?"

"That I could sleep in the gullers' tent."

"All right," Emmy said with a wink. "Tonight,

after you are full of lobsters and clams, you can go off and sleep with Bill and Gary."

"Yikes!" Ricky cried, and scampered along the beach with Blackie yapping at his heels.